Contents

Copyright

©

SECRETARY'S
obsession

LISA OLIVER & JP SAYLE

Secretary's Obsession

An overly dramatic pale blue demon. A bear who is hiding from his past. A big dose of miscommunication. Will these two make it work or has Fate finally gotten it wrong?

Scott, personal secretary to Dakata, is excellent at his job because Scott needs to be in control of *everything*. When sent to visit an injured taxi driver in the hospital—his blissful one—Scott discovers the true meaning of losing control when his demon—who has never been on a rampage in his life—loses it when their blissful one disappears. Now Scott is about to learn just how out-of-control life really is when his dramatic demon wants his say.

George, a bear minding his own business, hiding—living his life the way he wants away from a clan that had one use for him, a sperm doner, never expects to find his mate. Only the accident gives George more than a mate, it puts him back in crosshairs of his clan.

Now the pair must figure out how to be together, while Scott's family is not accepting of their bond and George's past looms out of the shadows. Easy? They are about to find out!

Secretary's Obsession is book four in the Obsession series, proving that meeting a blissful one can upend a demon's life and make it infinitely better.

Dedication

Dedication Lisa Oliver

Sending love and hugs to our wonderful friends who enjoy these stories. Remember love wins, my friends, and don't forget to hug the ones you love xx

Dedication JP Sayle

I'm never sure where we are heading when we start writing, and sometimes the surprise is so much better than I expect, thank you to everyone who comes on our journey.

Chapter One

Scott

Brushing back his hair, Scott listened to Christa with half an ear, that was all he needed because he could easily keep up. His fingers flew over the iPad. He was taking notes for the concert that required organizing for the latest up-and-coming band. The music wasn't to Scott's taste, but he could understand the human appeal when the band was made up of handsome men in their early twenties.

"We need to speak to Vince and ask if we can have the venue for an additional night because the tickets sold out in three minutes, and the demand suggests it would be financially worthwhile."

Scott nodded, making an additional note to contact Vince. As a multitasker, Scott had learned long ago how to focus and prioritize what he needed to do first.

Dakata, a demon friend of his family, had built his music business from the ground up. When Scott had heard him complaining to his father about struggling to find someone in the human realm who was equipped to deal with Dakata's demands, Scott had offered to work for Dakata. Even though his family had scoffed at him, he excelled and had quickly become Dakata's right-hand demon.

Scott now knew the business inside out. Loved how he could slot all the pieces together to assist in making a band, or an event, reach its full potential.

"Are you listening to me?" Christa, Dakata's sister, questioned, one shapely brow arched to perfection while she swept her black flowing locks over one shoulder.

"Of course." Christa and her brothers did not focus on the details like Dakata, which was irritating, to say the least. Scott liked things organized and was not used to this current chaotic state the office was in.

But since Dakata had met his blissful one, which most demons, himself included, thought was more of a myth, things had changed. Scott had hardly recovered from the shock when Merihem, Dakata's best friend—who had become forced by the Demon King to come and work for Dakata because of a minor issue in the demon realm—had found his blissful one, too.

It was as if it was catching...

"Are you going to go? It seems rather urgent?" Christa's voice penetrated past his thoughts, and he kept his expression totally neutral at being caught—for the first time—not paying attention.

He stared at Christa, hoping to gauge what he'd missed. When he got nothing, he ignored the smug smile at not being able to read her and swallowed his sigh of frustration.

"Merihem reached out. He's been in an accident—"

"What!" Up off the seat, his concern for Merihem, who he genuinely liked, his sleeping demon stirred for the first time that day. His demon side hated office work so much that he spent most of the day sleeping when Scott was at work.

"He's fine, as is Peni. They need you to go to them because of the cab driver, George, he needs to go to the hospital," Christa explained as she wrote on a piece of paper.

A moment later, she pushed it over the table towards him, and he picked it up, seeing an address for a street he didn't believe was that far away. He gave her a searching look, his concern for those he knew well held in check.

He didn't jump to conclusions. "This cab driver, why is he important?"

Christa's expression grew grave, and Scott's demon paid attention. "He is a friend of Silas's and injured seriously enough that he isn't able to shift to heal. Merihem wants to ensure he's looked after. Can you do that?"

"Of course."

"Get him whatever he needs," Christa added, like Scott needed the added instructions, when he didn't.

Scott used his iPad to search for the details of the nearest hospital to where the accident was, working out the logistics. He often chose not to translocate, he much preferred human travel. It was less taxing when his demon wasn't always awake.

The movement of Christa sitting back in her seat, crossing a silk-clad leg over the other, got Scott meeting her gaze. A light of amusement was there in the depth of her eyes. "Are you going? He's unconscious and has no one to advocate for him." She pointed at his tablet. "What are you doing?"

"He may have healed before I get there. But I'm looking at the hospitals in the area, assessing likely courses of action for the paramedics." Shifters, like demons, had the ability to heal themselves. The bear would probably be gone before Scott got there. Clearly, it was going to be a waste of his time.

He expressed none of his thoughts on the matter, while he considered what he would have to shuffle around to make sure he met all the personal deadlines he set himself to keep everything in order.

Christa gave him a seductive smile, one that would never work on Scott, as he wasn't interested in females or dating another demon. They were all arrogant, and he'd had enough of that to last him a lifetime with his family. He liked calm and orderly, not chaotic or rampaging. It just wasn't him.

"Possibly, but our guys are worried about the bear, so just check on them and him. I'll sort through what's needed here, so don't worry." She clearly got what his reluctance was. Christa or her brothers had no talent for organization, to Scott's mind.

He nodded, spun around on his Italian loafers, and left the room, keeping the worry about how she'd achieve the things on the long list he'd established to keep her on track. When Christa went off in the opposite direction from

Scott's way of working, it was troublesome. But he got paid handsomely, so he didn't complain.

At his desk, he tidied everything away in its place and tucked the iPad in his laptop bag. He would work at the hospital while they did whatever was needed so as not to waste time.

Scott released a quiet sigh at thoughts of this disruption and messaged Dakata's driver.

With his laptop bag slung over his broad shoulder, two minutes later he slipped out of the building. Dakata's car and driver were waiting for him. He moved swiftly and got into the back seat, the scent of leather greeting his nose. He settled back and immediately pulled out his laptop, resting it on his knees before giving the street address to the driver.

Minutes passed, and Scott lost track of time as he sent emails and re-organized his workload. When he glanced up as the car slid to a stop next to a police car, he looked at the scene of carnage. His pulse leaped at the mangled car.

Seeing Merihem holding a small goat, Scott tucked his laptop away and got out of the car, striding past the wreckage, and considered that Merihem and Peni were lucky to escape.

As he passed the ambulance, he noted the doors shutting as he reached Merihem. He saw a glimpse of a person on a trolley inside.

He'd barely come to a stop when Merihem demanded, "Scott, give this officer details of where to find me." There was no waiting for a reply, Merihem stalked off with his blissful one in his arms.

Scott offered a polite smile, pulling out a card from his wallet. "You can contact this number, and I will organize a suitable time to discuss the accident."

Scott didn't acknowledge the blustering officer, he just repeated himself once more before leaving to go back to the car when the ambulance sirens blared as it drove off.

There were several bleats coming from Peni when Scott got into the back of the car. Seated, he glanced at Merihem. "Where to?" Scott tugged on the cuff of his suit jacket, crossing his legs.

"Take us to Dakata's house."

Scott gave the instructions to the driver while he listened to Merihem work to coax Peni to shift into his human form.

Scott watched in fascination when a rather giddy goat attempted to climb Merihem's chest.

When they came to a stop, Merihem looked flushed, and his efforts to get Peni to shift had been unsuccessful.

"I need you to follow up with George, the cab driver. Go to the hospital and pay any bills for his care. See that they look after him."

Scott nodded, knowing already that would be his next task. "Of course."

Merihem got out of the car, buck naked. Scott heard a woman walking past gasp. Peni bleated and kicked his hooves in the woman's direction when she stopped to stare.

Scott held back a chuckle when he heard Merihem whisper, "That told her," which earned him a lick to his face from the goat.

When Merihem returned his attention to the open door and Scott, he grinned. "I'll not be in the office for the rest of the week. Can you email me everything you want me to look at and courier over anything requiring signing?"

"Of course."

Back with his laptop on his knee, Scott pulled up a schematic of the emergency department while tracking the ambulance via the street cameras. Not strictly legal, but it allowed him to know exactly where George was and would end up.

When they stopped behind the same ambulance, Scott closed down his laptop and set it aside. "Please find somewhere to wait, I'll call you when I'm ready to leave."

"Yes, sir."

Out of the car, Scott strode into the emergency room, his nose twitched at the scents assaulting him. He went to the desk where people stood queuing. He patiently waited his turn.

The woman behind the counter didn't even bother to look at him as he stepped forward. "How can I help you?" she asked in a bored tone.

"I'm looking for George Maybank. He was brought in after an accident involving several people."

"Are you a relative?" She tapped at the keyboard.

"Yes," he lied, not wanting to explain why he was there or who had sent him.

Gum moved its way around her teeth as she blew a bubble, and it popped as she finally glanced at him. When she got a look at him, the bored look disappeared. A smile appeared, he supposed she thought was flirty.

His blond good looks and dimples often got this reaction. "He's in the emergency bay for assessment and observation."

"Thank you." He spun about and walked off, not needing anything more.

"Sir, you can't go back there," she called after him.

He merely nodded to confirm he'd heard her and continued on. He glanced about, looking for a place to translocate, unobserved into the emergency department.

He followed the signs and stepped into a side ward, then gave himself a moment to think about what he'd seen on the schematic before he translocated. No one noticed his arrival. How would they when it looked like a demon had been through the area on a rampage?

People moved franticly, darting past obstacles as they went about their business. Twice he tried to attract someone's attention and then gave up.

He walked to the electronic board that displayed patients' names and locations. He noted the one he needed and easily found the cubicle.

Scott glanced about, listening when he came to a stop at a half-drawn curtain around a gurney with a large pair of booted feet hanging off the end.

Scott's demon chose then to wake up fully. *Why are we in a smelly hospital? And who is that little honey?*

Little honey? To whom are you referring?

His demon side chuckled at him. *You need to remove that stick from your ass occasionally.*

Behave.

Hey, I'm just saying it how it is. And who is the honey bear?

Scott glanced at the gurney, not quite seeing a honey bear, but then his demon could be whimsical occasionally. *He's a friend of Silas.*

The enormous man smelled like a bear, but there was no sweet honey smell. Dark, wavy brown hair hung around a rugged face. A wound to the left side of his head showed why he was there. The black and purple bruising didn't detract from how handsome he was.

Handsome.

Maybe he'd taken a hit to the head! Or maybe his demon was pushing the thought into his head?

He's sexy, his demon purred, and Scott rolled his eyes heavenward.

You think any guy with legs is sexy. It was the truth.

The chuckling continued in his mind and made Scott reluctant to see what his demon would do when he got closer. But he had a duty to check on the bear, and that's what he would do.

Stepping behind the curtain, Scott caught a flicker of eyelid movement from the bear. His body froze and something flowed through him, an awareness that made him hyper-alert and attuned to his demon. Something that so rarely happened, he braced—for what he couldn't say—as he watched those eyes move with a sense of dread.

When they fluttered open, Scott forced his lips into a smile to give reassurance because he didn't need the bear freaking out on him. Only the moment their eyes connected, Scott's demon, who was not one to be a nuisance or cause trouble, wanted out. He surged so hard that if not for the gurney in front of him, he'd have been forcibly thrown to the ground. Instead, Scott had to reach out and grab the rail to stay upright.

He panted, his insides spiraling out of control at the need from his demon side to touch the bear. His hands clawed as he struggled to hold back.

What on earth is wrong with you?

Ours!

Chapter Two

George

Damn fucking useless demons. George struggled to wake up. Yes, he knew he'd been in an accident. He wasn't going to forget that maniac demon deliberately driving into his taxicab in a hurry. He knew he was in a hospital. His nose still worked, and he could smell the stench of illness and disinfectant—it was enough to give him a headache, and that was without the blow he'd taken to the head when his cab flipped. He also knew, and that was the biggest kicker of all, that someone, goodness knows who, had fucking injected him to stop him from shifting, and when George got his hands on that person...

Shifting was crucial to his damn healing process. Didn't anyone teach modern doctors anything anymore?

Open, open, open. George willed his eyes to freaking open and focus. There was someone close, someone who smelled incredible, but George had other matters to deal with.

When he finally got his eyes to work—yay, step fucking one—George glared at a smartly dressed cutie resting his hands on the rail of his bed.

"Who the hell are you?" he demanded in a too pissed off to care tone.

"Not from hell, actually." The well-dressed man had an incredibly soothing voice. "Demon realm. It's different."

"I know it's fucking different. I asked who the hell you were and what you're doing here? Are you going to finish me off? Checking to see if the demon that wrecked my car had done his job properly? Well, guess what? He fucked up. I'm still alive, and I want to know who the hell you are, Mr. Demon Realm."

And stop smelling so damn sexy. George didn't have time for that shit. For all he knew, the demon just looked good because he'd had a severe blow to the head.

The man-demon did a funny tilt thing, as if he had a crick in his neck, and then said, "I'm Scott. I work for Dakata's organization. Merihem, the demon in the taxi with you, asked me to come here, make sure you're being taken care of, and ensure all the bills get paid in full."

"Well, that's the first bit of good news I've had today." George shifted on the bed, trying to sit up.

Scott was hovering, and George really didn't think he'd be able to contain himself if the demon touched him, so he glared until he was sitting under his own steam. "I probably shouldn't have snapped. Not having the best of days. Seriously, you're here to help me out?"

"Whatever you need. I'm authorized to take care of everything."

George became fascinated when Scott nodded, and barely a hair on his head moved. It was like someone had glued it to his head. A very sexy head... *Fucking stop it.*

"Right." George swallowed, his nose wrinkling as he tasted his own blood. "I'm a bit banged up, but somebody, and I have no idea who, has fucking shot me up with shit to stop me shifting."

"You can't shift?" Scott's pretty blue eyes widened. "How can you heal if you can't shift?"

That's when George noticed the dimples. *I am so doomed. Doomed, I tell you. Doomed.* "Bingo. I guess I'll heal just like anyone else in this godforsaken place—not very well. Look, if you want to do something for me, then go investigate..." He flapped both hands in Scott's direction. "Someone on the paramedic team knew I was a shifter—using shifter drugs on a human would kill them. So how the hell did they know that? I was unconscious, so it's not like I could tell them. Someone wanted me in this hospital, and I have no idea why. So, you go and find out why I'm here, and I'll work on getting this shit they've doped me up with out of my system."

Scott just blinked and then blinked again. "At the risk of upsetting you, that sounds a bit like a conspiracy theory. Why would anyone want you in a hospital?"

"Maybe they want to harvest my organs. There's another conspiracy theory for you to investigate." George rested his hands on his knees, leaning forward, knowing that would bulge out his biceps. Yes, he was trying to look intimidating, but he needed the sexy-looking demon out of his space, or he wouldn't be responsible for his actions. "I don't know, but I *do* care. You said you're here to help me, so unless you're going to help me get out of this damn bed and out of this cursed place…?"

Scott shook his head. "You've got blood," he fluttered his hand in George's direction. "All over your face, and bruises, too. You haven't seen a doctor yet. At least do that before you try to leave."

Fucking knew it. George was not pouting. He'd never pouted in his life, but that didn't mean he didn't want to stamp his feet, which he couldn't do because he was on a damn bed, and Scott the demon was making him think things he didn't have the brainpower for with the thumping going on in his skull.

"Then I'm asking you," he said with a low growl, "asking as nicely as I can, considering I was in a car accident. Would you please go and find out why I'm here, who authorized that, and find out who the hell drugged me? Can you do that? Would you do that for me?"

Scott's eyes flickered between George and the curtain. "I can do that, but wouldn't you rather—"

"No, no." George shook his head and then reached up and rubbed it. His fingers came away covered in road grit and blood. "I don't need you to do anything else." *Honestly, if that sweet thing offers to rub my head or any part of me, I will not be held responsible.* "Please. Go and check out my paperwork. I want the name of that paramedic. And while you're at it, if you can find out where my taxicab got taken, because that's important to me…"

"If you're sure it will help."

"It will. It will. You'd be reducing my stress levels, and that has to be a good thing, right?"

"Right. All right." Clearly, Scott had come to a decision because he tugged on one of the cuffs of his jacket and straightened his spine. "I won't be long. I'll be right back."

"Just get the information. Thank you." George watched as Scott ducked around the curtain, listening as he heard the expensive shoes make their way down the hallway. It was only then that he glared at his crotch. *As if that hot sweetie would have anything to do with the likes of you.*

George had more important things to worry about than a hard-on that was showing no signs of going down. *I've got to get out of here.* He'd only been joking about organ harvesting, but the drugging was real. He could feel it moving sluggishly through his system. His bear was fighting it, but it might not be soon enough if someone came after him while he was hopeless in bed.

I'm not hopeless.

I'm not helpless.

I can fucking do this.

Swinging his legs off the side of the bed, George was grateful he still had his clothes and boots on. Patting his pocket, his eyes widened as he felt his wallet was still in there. *They didn't want to rob me then.*

Shuffling over to the curtain, George peeked out. The place was busy, people rushing up and down, buzzers buzzing, beepers blaring, and someone talking over the speaker system, calling doctors and nurses to various rooms.

Just look like you know where you're going, he thought as he stepped out. George knew he looked a fright on a good day. The bruises and blood all down his face weren't going to make him look any better.

Head up, he strode down the hall in the opposite way he'd heard Scott going. There was a door marked "Exit" and that's all he needed. His head still pounding and his cock still hard, George made his escape. With any luck, there'd be a taxicab waiting on the rank alongside the hospital.

It crossed George's mind, as he was being driven away from the hospital, that if he hadn't gotten drugged, then his bear wouldn't have let him leave that cutie demon behind, even if George knew it was for the best. *I've had more than enough shit to deal with today. Being rejected by my mate can wait for another time, preferably after I've healed.*

Chapter Three

Scott

Leaving was the last thing he'd wanted to do, but with his demon insistent that the large, scruffy bear was theirs, Scott had taken matters into his own hands. It was that or do something he'd struggled to stop happening, his demon coming out to play.

Outside the curtain, he took a deep breath and regretted it at the stench of blood and guts coming from somewhere to his left. He walked in the opposite direction, searching for someone that smelled like a shifter to gain some answers for George. Hopefully, that would settle the bear, who seemed to have a few issues.

He has no issues whatsoever, it's you that is the problem.

What is up with you? Scott asked his demon side impatiently, still dealing with the whole 'blissful one' possibility.

He's ours, and no pretending will convince me or him otherwise. Don't deny you can't feel the need to touch... to taste that gorgeous honey bear.

That 'gorgeous honey bear' couldn't wait for us to leave him alone. What of that suggests he knows he belongs to us? Because if this were real, he motioned with his fingers, *then as a shifter, he'd know it, too.* The moment Scott considered that and how the bear had behaved, his shoulders slumped, and to distract himself from the dull ache in his chest, he looked about to find someone to ask the questions *their bear* wanted answering.

Told you.

Be quiet!

"Excuse me, could you help me?" Scott asked of the first person who wasn't running.

The woman in navy scrubs eyed him with impatience as she moved the tray she held into her other hand away from him. Did she think he was interested in taking her drugs?

He felt the insult and stood a little taller, straightening his suit jacket and then his tie.

"What is it you need?" She scanned his suit before looking him in the eye, but nothing changed in her expression.

A furrow appeared on the bridge of his nose as he stared her down. "George Maybank, the bear shifter in the cubicle just down there in the emergency bay needs some attention and has questions relating to why the paramedics took it upon themselves to drug him to prevent him from shifting and healing."

As Scott considered that George had been left alone with a head injury, his anger, something he rarely felt, surfaced at the lack of care. "Does this hospital not cater to shifters? Consider them as second-class citizens? The man has been seriously injured. He has a head injury that has him talking about conspiracy theories." Scott didn't know if that was George's usual behavior, but he was gaining a head of steam now and couldn't stop. "You have left him alone. Why is that? To me, it appears his care needs aren't equivocal to others in the department." He inhaled to assess exactly how many non-humans were in the department.

"I-I think y-you should calm down, or I'll need to get security," the nurse stammered, taking a step back.

Scott, in the right frame of mind, might have agreed. He wasn't in any frame of mind for listening to nonsense. He'd have to think about that later.

"That's fine, and while we are at it, we can call the police too, and I can get them to come and arrest you for aiding and abetting whoever hurt George." Words tumbled from his lips, and Scott became horrified but unable to stop.

He could see he'd lost her to fear. A human response: they had merged care facilities years ago, yet places like this weren't equipped enough to deal with shifters or a very upset demon.

"You'll need to wait for the shifter doc. He's busy with another patient right now. As you can see, we're busy. There are other sick patients that are triaged and have taken priority over the bear," she fired back unprofessionally in Scott's opinion, not that he could point fingers when he wasn't acting like his usual self.

He had no time to continue the argument and stab his point home because she bustled off so fast that her scrub pants flapped about her legs.

How long would the doctor be?

Minutes?

Hours?

Their bear needed to be treated now. Those drugs...

We need to get our bear out of here. His conspiracy theories could have some genuine merit.

He didn't want to agree with his demon half, but his gut was churning at the lack of care George had gotten since he'd arrived. *Don't be ridiculous. Who would want to harm a simple cab driver?*

Whoever crashed into his cab.

Scott paused at the icy feeling spreading down his spine at how he'd gotten lost in staring at the bear, that he'd actually lost the thread of what he'd said. Now as he ran back over it, he recalled George pointedly saying a demon had wrecked his car. Had someone known that the bear was a blissful one and wanted to harm him?

He shuddered, and his demon was back to being a pushy asshole. *Go back to him, now. He's not safe in here.*

Stop. We need to find the doctor, get him to do his assessment, and give George something to reverse the drugs so he can shift and heal. Then the doctor can check if he's better and only when that happens will we ask to take him home.

Can you hear yourself?

I haven't lost my hearing, Scott snapped back impatiently, feeling out of sorts at the lack of control he felt. It was a position he hated to be in. It was just the lack of care that was pissing him off. Shifters needed someone to speak up for them.

Just go back, I'm worried for our blissful one. One of us has to be.

The snide comment made Scott snarl. The person heading towards them gave him an alarmed look and changed direction. Scott took a deep breath and swung around, heading back to where George was. *I hope you're happy. We have no answers to give our bear. Let's see how he feels about that.*

He'll just be happy to see us, he won't care.

Back outside the cubicle, Scott took a moment to compose himself. He straightened his tie and tugged on the cuffs of his suit jacket, then smoothed over his hair. He rolled his shoulders back and put on his best smile as he stepped once more behind the curtain. Blinking, he stared dazedly at the empty trolley.

Blood smeared the pillow, and the scent of bear, *their bear,* said he was in the right place.

Someone must have taken him for a head scan.

Are you sure? Maybe someone kidnapped him.

Back to shuddering at how worried his demon sounded. *What did I say about being ridiculous? Clearly, you are acting like the bear with your conspiracy theories.*

A demon crashed into his car!

Fuck!

He spun around so fast he could have left a scorch mark on the tiled floor and marched back out, his ears buzzing with how hard his heart was beating as he scented the air, looking for the direction the bear had gone in. The whole time, his fists clenched as if that would stop his demon from emerging.

He'd barely made it to the door that said 'Exit' before his demon managed to rip control from him. He emerged with a roar, tearing the door from its hinges, throwing it away like a twig as he charged after the scent of their bear.

Pale blue, his demon side was prettier than most, and part of the reason he had issues with his family. He looked nothing like them, and others had often ridiculed him because he was paler than most other blue demons.

Those in the stairwell gasped as he raced to find George and rescue him from whatever idiot had taken him. His beautiful suit was torn and flapping about his body, but Scott had no time to fret about that when they reached the street and found George's scent stopped at the curbside.

Head thrown back, blond hair cascading over his pale blue shoulders, his demon roared its fury for the world to hear.

We'll get arrested if you don't stop that. I also can't think, and we need one part of us to be sensible.

He's gone. Someone has our bear!

We won't be able to find him in a police cell, will we? Scott questioned, trying to quell his own anxiety. *Let's go back to the office and see what Christa knows about George. We can also reach out to Silas and Dakata. They'll help us.*

The roaring stopped, and his demon stomped back to the car, everyone giving them a wide berth. At the car, Scott heard sirens in the distance. He forced his demon side into the car and slammed the door. He took a moment and used considerable effort to get his demon to recede.

The driver gave him a comical, wide-eyed stare in the rearview mirror. Not that Scott could see the funny side of anything right then. No one had seen his demon side in years. "Take us back to the office, but first, we need to go back via my home to grab a suit." He glanced down at what remained of his Italian handmade clothes and groaned.

You can replace a suit, but we can't replace our blissful one!

His demon was right. It was, however, a damn sight easier to think about his suit than failing his blissful one when the ache in his chest was making it hard to breathe. *Had someone kidnapped their blissful one? Taken him to…*

A violent shudder rocked him in the leather seat. "Hurry," he barked at the driver, "and keep an eye out for demons in cars." He'd need to talk to Merihem, too, he had to know something… surely?

Chapter Four

George

"I'm fairly sure that tree didn't do anything to you. Is there a reason why you're banging your head into it like you're trying to knock it down?"

George, still in bear form, glared at his friend. Dougal was a troll and had been with the forest since it was a half a dozen shoots, hoping to become something substantial. He and Dougal had spent many happy hours sitting around the campfire, shooting shit about nothing at all, and George always appreciated the friendship. Dougal was one person who was not put off by his brusque manner.

"Word on the wind is that your cab got totaled by a random demon with a grudge against Merihem after he found his blissful one."

That had George sitting back on his haunches, his head tilted.

Realization blossomed all over Dougal's face. "Oh, shit George. Did you think the accident had something to do with *before*?"

The *before* times were something George spilled his guts about one night after too much shifter booze. Only to Dougal, only the once, and they'd never spoken about it since. For Dougal to bring it up now...

Sighing, George realized there was a shit ton of things he couldn't say in his bear form, so he shifted. "Pass me my pants," he grumbled, rubbing his head with his hand. It wasn't as bad as it was before the shift, although hitting the tree with it probably hadn't helped. But the drugs were now fully out of his system.

"You can't blame me for thinking that," he said as he lifted one foot and then the other, stepping into pants still covered in road grime. "You're saying the attack was leveled at Merihem?"

"Drink this." Dougal shoved a steaming cup into his hand. "Have a seat."

George parked his butt on a fallen log while Dougal sat beside him.

"According to the word flying around the forest, Merihem was the target of the demon who smashed into your cab. The guy was the one who has taken over Merihem's position in the demon realm, although from what I've heard, Merihem will be getting his position back before long."

Not for the first time, George wondered where Dougal got his information from, but his friend had never been wrong before, especially about the demon realm.

"Doesn't make any difference to me, does it?" George took a swig from his mug and then stared at the dark liquid. "My cab's still smashed up, someone filled me full of a non-shifting drug, landing me in hospital, and…"

"What the fuck? You were drugged?"

"See," George pointed at Dougal, "You understand. Yes, I was drugged. Someone at the accident scene knew I was a shifter. I wasn't in any state to say anything, so god knows how they knew, but the moment I regained consciousness, my bear should've taken over and helped me heal. Instead, I wake up in a piss-ass hospital bed, separated from everyone else by a fucking curtain, with my feet falling over the edge of the bed, my body fighting the drugs, and not an ounce of care in sight."

"How did they know? For all intents and purposes, when the paramedics arrived, if anything, they should've given you something to help you shift at the scene—a shot of adrenalin or something. You'd have healed and gone on your merry way. Most shifters never see the inside of a hospital."

"There you go. That's what I thought. So, was it any wonder I think something else is going on?"

"Perhaps the paramedic was a shifter," Dougal offered. "They could've scented you were a shifter and even what type."

George snorted. "What paranormal in any occupation would willingly drug a fellow shifter to stop them shifting when they needed to heal? What if my bear had come through in a human hospital? Think about what would've happened if I'd shifted before I was fully conscious. Trapped in a tiny room with no privacy and all those horrible smells...my bear would've run amuck, probably leaving a half a dozen patients with heart attacks as he tried to find a way out. It's why shifters don't belong in the hospital in the first place."

"Is it possible they thought you'd sustained a more serious injury, perhaps?"

"I had a head injury. The cab flipped, and I went with it. I have a strong suspicion I owe that demon Merihem thanks for pulling me out, but still, a head injury for a shifter does not require a hospital visit."

"That does sound strange then, but how would anyone from before know it was you in the cab?"

Scratching the side of his head, George grimaced. "We have to provide proof of ID when we get a license to run a cab in the first place. They could've tracked that. I accept, okay, from what you've said that was no bloody accident, and that it happened because of Merihem. What if someone else was waiting in the wings for an opportunity, and when they saw I was unconscious, they ran with it?"

"Still doesn't explain the hospital."

"Actually, yes, it does." George resisted the urge to grab his balls and make sure they were still intact. "Where better to harvest my spunk and insert it in someone else?" He sighed. "Okay, I'm probably growling up the wrong tree, but it's all damn weird, and then with that cutie demon just standing there—"

"You got a cutie demon as a nurse, and you still escaped?" Dougal grinned. "You must've hit your head harder than I thought."

"He wasn't a nurse. Apparently, he works for Dakata, and can I just say he must be on a damn good salary because I'm sure his suit cost more than my cab."

"Most demons dress like that." Dougal laughed. "What was he doing at your bedside if he works for Dakata? Was he making sure you weren't going to sue Merihem or something?"

"Merihem sent him." *See, he hadn't actually come to see you, he was following orders.* "Apparently, Merihem was well enough after the crash to tell Scott to take care of my account at the hospital and anything else I needed."

"Very accommodating of them, but then Silas and Dakata truly appreciate you, as do the rest of us who live here. I hope you know that."

George glanced across at his friend. "What did you put in this coffee? For a moment, I could swear you were handing out compliments."

"Where was the first place you thought to run to when you escaped the hospital? Not your house, but the forest," Dougal countered. "You're as much a part of this place as I am."

"My bear needed out and my neighbors complain if I do that in my yard," George grumbled, although he knew his friend was right.

"Whatever you need to tell yourself," Dougal shifted his weight on the log. "So, what happened to the cutie demon? Did he just run off and pay your account the moment you said you wanted to leave?"

"I sent him off on a fool's errand," George mumbled into his mug. "The cutie demon's my mate, and we both know, you and me,"—he indicated the space between his chest and Dougal's—"we know a guy like him is never going to accept someone like me. We both know it, so don't deny it. Just don't. I couldn't handle getting rejected by my mate on the same day my cab got wrecked. I just couldn't, so I snuck out and left him there chasing down my conspiracy theories—and that's what he called them, not me, not at first anyway."

Dougal frowned, tapping his chin. "If this cutie demon is your mate, then you're his blissful one."

"Yeah. So?"

"Hmm, nothing. It's just that word on the wind is that the king of the demon realm, Asmodeus, has got a real hard-on about his demons finding their blissful ones at the moment."

"I sometimes think your wind talks too much," George grumped. "You don't have to give me some song and dance about how a mate is the most important person in a shifter's life, and how once they're together, nothing will ever break them apart. I'll tell you what will keep me and Scott apart..." He pointed to his face. "This face." His hand moved. "This body." Then his hand went wide. "This scruff and my size."

He continued, making sure to get his point across about all the differing bits he mentioned. "I drive a cab for a living, or at least I used to. You didn't see him. The creases on his clothes were so sharp they could cut someone. He was wearing fancy shoes from Europe. He had one of those body bags slung across his shoulders, and it didn't leave a crease anywhere on his body. Did you know... did you know..." George was on a roll, determined his friend would understand.

"Scott nodded, right? He nodded at me at one point, and barely a hair on his head moved. It was so stylish and well cut." *Beautiful.* But George kept that part to himself. "There is nothing on this earth, or the demon realm for that matter, that would convince that demon to care one fig about a rough vagabond like me. Nothing."

"I don't think that's how it works with mates and bliss-ful ones," Dougal said slowly. "If he doesn't come after you, your bear is going to be running off to Dakata's office building every chance he gets."

"Why do you think I was banging my head against a tree?" George slumped off the log, sitting his ass on the ground and leaning back against the wood. "I know he's mine, but from what I've seen, the kindest thing I could do for him is stay out of his way. My bear will understand that in time."

"Or not." Dougal held up a flask. "Did you want more coffee?"

George held out his mug. With his taxi gone, it's not like he had anywhere else he had to be.

Chapter Five

Scott

Dressed at record speed, Scott left the remnants of his suit in a bag for disposal when he had more time. On the drive back to the office, he used the time to do something productive. He searched the internet for George Maybank, only to come up with bupkiss on anyone with that name.

How could the bear have no information on the internet? Everyone left a trace somewhere on the web. Frustration levels reached an all-time high for Scott, who, somewhere between his demon acting out and losing their blissful one, had found he wasn't as calm and collected as he thought.

So, when he stepped into the elevator and encountered the dweeb Dervis from accounting, he struggled not to groan at his misfortune. The man didn't get Scott wasn't interested, and his tolerance for small talk was at an all-time low.

"Did you see the forecast for Demon's Blessing? They are really going to boost the dividends this month."

Scott nodded.

"The bonuses will surely help towards the last payment on my Bugatti."

Did he think any of this conversation was scintillating? The guy had flirted with Scott once or twice at work functions. He smelled funky and had a habit of picking his teeth.

Who did that in public?

Scott gave another nod at the suitable time, or he thought he did. His mind was more occupied with what he wanted. George.

He needed to get out of this damn elevator and contact Dakata and Silas, maybe even Merihem, to figure out how to find George. Although, as Merihem had entrusted him to look after George's needs, it wouldn't do to say he'd left the hospital having not done that. He'd not even gone and paid the hospital bill, something he would need to rectify once he was in his office because he'd just remembered that.

Where had George gone? Had he gone willingly? Was he alright? Had he managed to shift and get the drugs out of his system?

More questions, all of which increased the need for his demon side, who wanted to veer towards starting a rampage to find their bear.

Behave. We have to figure this out sensibly.

What did that do for us the last time? Our bear is missing.

Do you need to fucking shout at me? I know he's missing.

The doors opened, and Scott stepped out, not seeing the other guy staring open-mouthed from his rudeness. He strode with purpose into his office. The man in the elevator, not anywhere on his radar, when he placed his laptop bag down and headed back out into the corridor, walking straight to Dakata's—Christa's office.

He didn't so much as hesitate to knock; he had no time to waste.

Christa glanced up, a frown tugging at her sculpted brows. "When did you ever enter an office without knocking? And why aren't you at the hospital?"

The snap to her tone that could flay skin from bone, Scott didn't notice. He jabbed a finger at her. "I went to the hospital, and the bear is gone. I need to find him!"

Christa lounged back in her seat. "I feel I'm missing something here?" Her expression revealed her interest.

"Does Dakata have the cab driver's contact information?" he asked, ignoring her inquiring stare.

"I have no idea." Her perfect bow lips pulled into a thoughtful pout. "You'll have to ask him yourself." She tapped her painted nails on the arm of the chair. "In fact, why don't we both take a trip to the forest to talk to Dakata *in person*?"

"What? Why do you need to come?" Scott questioned, his scrambled thoughts giving him no clue as to why he'd need an escort. As far as Scott was aware, Christa didn't like nature or going places with more foliage and fewer creature comforts. Scott was aware they were more alike that he would ever admit.

She rose and smoothed down her dress down over her sumptuous curves as she came towards him. "I'm your boss—"

"No, Merihem is my boss after Dakata. You are an employee, the same as me." Scott had made this point before, Christa liked to quibble over such things.

Her laughter was bold as she slipped an arm through Scott's and turned him towards the door he'd come through. "You are too easy, you know that? That snooty tone gets me every time."

"I do not have a snooty tone," he argued, blocking his demon, who laughed as hard as Christa.

"You do, and you love to use it when you're annoyed. Like now." Somehow, she guided him back out of the building sans his laptop bag, something he never left work without. Into the back of the car, with Christa giving directions to the driver.

"I need my laptop!" Scott declared, hand going to the door handle.

Christa reached for his hand, removing it from the handle as the car pulled from the curb, not allowing him a chance to argue. "Do you sleep with the damn thing?"

Scott eyed Christa with a look that spoke volumes to his pissedoffness as he shook off her touch. "Of course not." He may have occasionally fallen asleep while working with the laptop on his lap. That did not count.

You keep believing that.

Give over, will you?

Whatever. Just find our bear, or I will.

You will not go on a rampage, do you hear me?

Play another demon tune, this one isn't jibing for me.

"What's wrong with you?" Christa tapped on Scott's forearm, bringing his attention to her.

"Nothing," he snapped back, then took a breath to calm himself. Today was not going according to any of his plans.

Our blissful one is not a plan, and you need to get your head out of your ass before we find him.

My head is most definitely not up my ass, Scott exclaimed, feeling affronted at the very thought.

See, this is what's wrong with you. You need to let loose a little.

Scott blocked his demon, this time with more force, as he'd had enough.

"Your demon side giving you a hard time?"

Christa's question was asked so quietly that Scott initially thought he had not heard her correctly. He met her gaze and something about her eyes suggested a sadness about her he'd never noticed before, so he answered honestly. "Yes."

"I feel you." Christa looked out the car window. "They don't always see that life isn't just black and white, that decisions come in an entire spectrum of colors that can make it hard to find the right one to fit."

Scott stared at Christa and got the distinct impression she wasn't actually talking to him at all. "Life can be more shades than we can fathom, yes."

She didn't turn to look at him as she nodded. "Absolutely true," she murmured quietly. "Then why can't others see that?"

Scott had no answer to that, so he reached into his suit jacket for his cell phone, only to come up empty-handed. His eyes widened. He never went anywhere without his phone! Never.

This is all your fault, he groused at his demon half.

Now you unblock me to bitch at me. Fuck you.

Well, I never!

I never… so get over yourself. You were as preoccupied as me, and with good reason.

When we find our bear you and I are going to have a serious conversation about your behavior.

The laughter was grating as the car slowed and they entered a rutted road that led to the drop-off place where Scott had traveled to see Dakata for work matters. He might not be so involved with everything, but that didn't mean Dakata trusted Merihem or his family. Scott never mentioned the trips here. That was up to Dakata.

The engine died and Christa didn't move from her position, giving Scott another feeling of disquiet that wasn't connected to him or George. "Are you okay?" Scott wasn't sure what compelled him to ask. Christa wasn't one to talk about anything personal with him, or anyone he was aware of, with maybe the exception of Dakata.

She didn't look at him as she reached for the door handle. "We'll see." On the cryptic note, she got out of the car. Shaking off his concern, Scott followed. He had bigger fish to fry.

Outside, his nose wrinkled as he inhaled, acclimatizing himself. Something he did every time because the smells were so different that he needed a moment to adjust. The familiar scents his nose filtered came with a surging demon, who roared, and Scott had no time to get hold of his demon half. Because even as he was cursing and worrying about another suit, it became just as torn as the one earlier. A pale blue demon, shredded clothes flapping around his body, his cock flapping about wildly, rampaged through the forest.

Creatures all scurried away as Scott's demon called to their blissful one. "George, my honey bear, call to me if you can. I'm coming, and I'll rip apart those who took you from us. I swear."

Dear demon gods! Why did I get you?

Chapter Six

George

"George, my honey bear…"

"Did you hear that?" Dougal lifted his head, his grin wide. "Someone's looking for their honey bear."

"Wait. What?" George was still nursing his headache, although it was getting better. One of the advantages of sitting with Dougal was the man didn't need to talk to provide company. "You think someone's looking for me?"

"Listen for yourself." Dougal got up. "I'm out of here. Sounds like someone's cutie demon thinks his honey bear has been taken against his will. I'm not going to try to explain to a bear's mate that they're so far off the mark it's not funny. Later."

"But I'm not a honey bear. Dougal, where are you going?" George half got up as Dougal disappeared but then sat down with a thunk as a blue demon came running into the clearing.

"Honey bear!" Arms wide open, the demon came crashing over, catching George in a hug that was impossible to get out of. He lifted George effortlessly off his log. "Oh, my goodness. I've been so worried, honey bear. Who took you? Why are you here? What are you doing in this place?"

"I'm not a honey bear." George tried pushing on the light blue shoulders, but the demon was impossible to move. "Scott, are you in there? Can you control your demon, please? You're squishing the air out of me."

"Goodness, yes. You've been hurt." Suddenly, the demon was sitting on the same log George had been on, and George was on his lap, being petted, gently, but being petted, nonetheless. "How's your poor head? Are you feeling okay? Should we go back to the hospital?"

"Scott? Are you in there?" George looked into the demon's, admittedly beautiful eyes.

"Oh, Scott's in there, don't mind him." The demon waved his hand, rolling his eyes. "He's twittering on about losing another suit, but what's a demon to do? You're our blissful one—so much more important than a suit. Scott's got a closet full of them."

George's heart sank, although his bear was in seventh heaven being coddled by their demon. "I don't think I own a suit," he said slowly.

"You don't need one. Who needs suits? If you want one, we'll get you one, but you, my lovely honey bear, are just perfect the way you are. Just look at you, with your cute beard and your lovely bushy hair." Patting hands followed the words on his beard and hair, making George worry about what else his demon might find perfect. "Ooh, I want to squish you so badly, my big honey bear."

"Are you sure you want to be with someone who looks like me?" George felt as if he was being squished already—between an overly enthusiastic demon and his bear who just wanted to come out and feel all that patting on his fur.

"Did someone make you feel bad about how you look?" The demon looked at him in shock. "How could anyone do that when you're the sexiest hunk I've ever seen? Who was it? Where are they?" The demon was looking around, one side and then the other, as though someone was standing by a tree, pointing and laughing at George.

"Not here," George said quickly. "No one here has ever said that. It's just, I know what I look like when I see my reflection in the mirror."

"Aww, my little honey bear suffers from low self-esteem." To George's shock and horror, he now had two demon hands framing his face, and his blue-skinned mate was dropping butterfly kisses all over his face. "I'll make you feel better about yourself. I'll tell you and show you how perfect and beautiful you are every day until you believe it."

"Okay, okay. I'm fine. Really, I'm fine." George wasn't sure whether to laugh or cry. Scott's demon was unlike any he'd ever met before. "You're stunning in either form. I'm just trying to be practical because I know I'm not."

"Practical, bah." At least the kissing stopped. Now George had to contend with having his face smushed by the demon's chest as he got hugged again. "You and Scott will get on fine. That man has turned being organized into a religion. But don't let him convert you. There's more to life than calendars and spreadsheets."

"Do I look very organized to you?" George laughed. "Look at me. My taxi's wrecked, I'm sitting shirtless in a forest, still wearing trousers covered in road grit and grease."

"Hmm. Where's your shirt?" The demon went back to looking around again. "I know you were wearing one at the hospital. Did the person who took you take it off you, ripping it apart at the seams in their mad desire to see your muscles? Who was it? I'll stamp their faces into the dirt for daring to lust over my blissful one like that."

"No one took me. I got a ride share to the forest from the hospital. My shirt and shoes are over there." George waved at a nearby tree. "I take my clothes off before I shift. My bear's body is so much bigger than mine, and I don't want to rip anything. It's typically what shifters do. Probably what demons should do, too?"

He gave a pointed look at his demon, who looked a bit shy, but with a hint of a pout. "You wouldn't like it if I ran around showing off my dick, would you?" Although, to be fair, George could say hand on heart, he'd never seen a pale blue dick before. It was pretty.

"I was in such a hurry to find you. Scott gets worried about dirt on his shoes and random bushes leaping out and ripping his clothes, but I knew we needed to find you because your honey bear would be missing us. He was missing us, wasn't he? That's why you were sitting there all alone, looking so sad."

How could George resist a face like that—one that looked so hopeful and yet so pleased with himself? It would take a stronger man than George to do it, so he didn't. "Me and my bear missed you from the moment you left the room at the hospital," he admitted.

"Then why…" Then the demon shook his head. "No, no. We don't need to know…"

"Yes, you do." It was George's turn to cup his demon's chin with both hands. "I thought I was doing right by you. I have a rather murky history. I rarely care what I look like, and there's not a person who's met me who would deny how grumpy I am on a good day. You're beautiful. In both forms. I thought… I believed I was doing the right thing by leaving you alone."

There was a long moment when the demon just looked at him so intently that George wanted to squirm—not something he could do seeing as he was literally sitting against his mate's dick.

"I get it," the demon said at last. "You had a head injury. That's fine, my cute little honey bear. I understand."

"You do know I'm not a honey bear, don't you? I'm a grizzly bear."

"A honey grizzly is still cute. You're my blissful one. I've got a blissful one. I'm so happy about it, I could dance."

"Not in the forest where anyone can see us. Not without clothes. Let me up a minute."

"Don't go far. I can run fast, you know."

"I'm just going over here." George went over to where his other clothes were in a pile on the ground. He slipped on his shoes, stuck his wallet in his pants pocket, and took his shirt back over to where the demon was now standing up, watching him. He quickly tied his shirt around the demon's waist so it covered most of his cute butt and dick. "I know demons can shift with clothes on," he said, tugging at the shirt until he was as happy as he could be. "Peni had Merihem doing it, so I know you can do it, too."

"Maybe." The demon swished his hips around, smiling at how the shirt went with him. "But this is nice. Thank you, my honey bear."

That's clearly going to be a work in progress. George caught the demon's hand, leading him towards the trail. "How did you get here? Do you have a car?"

"Dakata's driver, he'll still be waiting. Unless Christa took it..."

But no, as they got closer, George could see a car waiting. "Will Christa need a lift back to town?"

"She can translocate." The demon dived into the back seat of the car. "We'll take the car and let's go back to my place."

"We'll go back to mine," George said firmly, giving his address to the driver, who raised an eyebrow at Scott's appearance but just nodded when George told him where they wanted to go. "Bears have a need to see their mates in their own den," he added, answering the question he could see on the demon's face. *And at least I won't have to worry about messing anything up.*

Chapter Seven

Scott

Nervous, Scott had never been that in his life. He was a big, dangerous demon.

Can you hear yourself? You, a big dangerous demon. That is not what we are at all. Our honey bear wants to show us his den, so behave, or we're never going to get to the naked shimmy with our cutie.

Naked shimmy! Can you hear yourself? And what do you mean, behave? What are you insinuating?

That your anal-retentive behavior will piss off our bliss-ful one. He's already insecure about how he looks and dresses. Did you listen to him at all?

Of course I did!

Then don't go all clean freak on him. This is us getting cozy and—

I get the damn picture. Which means you need to stop being a bossy fucker and let me out.

Yeah, not so sure about that.

Do you think our honey bear wants to be having a 'naked shimmy' with your blue ass? It was a genuine question. They matched in size to their bear, and sex in their demon form was common practice when size wasn't an issue. Scott had years of ridicule about the color of his demon and wasn't comfortable showing his pale blue body, not even to his blissful one—or not yet. Even though he already had.

Didn't you see he wrapped his shirt around us so no one else got to see what we had to offer? He wants our blue ass for himself.

How do you know he wasn't just hiding it so others couldn't judge him for getting the blue reject?

A hand waved in front of their face, and they blinked at George, who had a wrinkle at the top of his nose that hadn't been there before. "You okay? You zoned out on me. I've been talking to you for the past minute."

Scott pushed his demon half aside and forcibly shifted, getting an amused look from his honey bear when he noted the suit he wore. "Sorry, we didn't mean to be rude. I was having a *discussion* with my demon." He kept his voice polite because he was sorry. He was showing a terrible example of poor behavior, and didn't want his blissful one to think he was rude.

Save me now! His demon did a dramatic slump, and Scott floundered when bushy brows arched up under messy bangs. Were those twigs in his hair?

Don't you dare start! His demon pushed to come back out and Scott felt sweat bead on his skin beneath his shirt.

"Are we gonna go into my place?"

Blushing, Scott glanced out the window, hanging on tooth and nail to his demon side to stop him from appearing. He nodded, feeling his hair fall messily around his face. This really was not how he wanted to present himself to his blissful one.

The enormous bear reached for the door handle, and a second later, bare-chested, he got out. Distracted by all the smooth, golden skin on show, Scott's body warmed in a fashion most definitely not suitable for a sidewalk. He groaned under his breath and pushed at his cock to make sure it didn't tent his trousers. The shirt their blissful one had given them sat under his ass.

George held the door and waited for Scott to exit. Scott felt his blush deepen as he gave George a shy smile at the gallant gesture. He exited, holding on to the shirt, keeping it in front of his slacks. He didn't sigh aloud at how his rearranging hadn't been successful because of his current situation, which was obvious because he was *harder* than ever before.

On the street, he looked up at the small house that had several window boxes outside full of flowers. The place, though a little shabby around the edges, spoke to Scott of a home well-loved. It appealed in ways he couldn't explain when he could smell his bear and the pretty flowers.

"This way," George rasped and sauntered to the front door.

Scott hesitated and then ducked his head back into the car. "I'll call you when I need you." Clueless how long they'd…

He shut the thought down when his ass clenched at the lack of knowledge about what George would expect from him. The car door clicked shut, and Scott took a deep breath, chasing after George.

Inside, George waited for him. The place smelled much the same as outside. Flowers and bear made for a heady combination when Scott closed the door behind him. Now he had the driving need to touch George. Only he wasn't sure how to go about that. Sex with strangers was far easier when they did it clothed and in a dark space, no one could see him.

"It's not much, but it's home," he muttered, sounding defensive.

See, he's picking up you're not impressed.

Honestly, you know I've said nothing, and I wasn't thinking about his home in that way.

You don't need to say a damn word!

You're making me nervous, stop it.

"Come in, I won't bite…" he swung around, his chest rippling and catching the light from a window, "unless you want me to," he said, chuckling.

Was that a question he should answer?

Could he be trying to break the ice? He'd seen his demon side naked, he knew what they looked like. Oh, to the demon gods, this was so hard to figure out!

"I was joking," George said after the silence went on for too long.

Scott was at a loss and flapped the hand holding the shirt around like he was trying to draw a bull to him. He found he couldn't look away from the intriguing man licking at full lips the bushy beard didn't conceal. Would it tickle his skin? "I don't mind if you like to bite," he blurted out, needing to say something.

So lame. What are you playing at?

Who the hell knows? he exclaimed, feeling completely out of sorts and unsure if letting his demon back out was the best course of action.

"Erm, right, yeah."

Was that a yes he liked to bite?

Quit with that and just get naked so we can—

Honestly, we need to get to know our blissful one.

That hard cock trying to escape those pressed pants says differently. I had him right where we wanted him, and you're ruining it.

"Can I have a cup of tea?" Scott felt his demon roll his eyes before he groaned.

"Right, a drink." George's brows rose, and his nose wrinkled. "Let's go through to the kitchen." He pointed down the small hallway to an open door, and Scott was back to staring at the magnificent chest he itched to touch. Scott tugged on his shirt collar, which felt way too tight around his neck.

Back to blushing, he seriously considered that he had no option but to let his demon out. He at least wasn't a total moron when it came to... *wooing our honey bear.*

He followed behind George, doing his best to keep his gaze from roaming down to the ass that his pants fitted snuggly. *That was not where I was going with that, and you know it.*

Let me out.

No. With how his demon was so focused on the naked parts of their bear, they would be naked before he could consider his next move.

You are, too.

Scott didn't feel his demon warranted an answer. It made sense to the rational side of him that he should be the one to remain in control. The last thing Scott wanted was to frighten off their bear again. He'd run before.

Scott eyed George, unsure of his moves. The bear had beautiful eyes. Should he say that? Would that encourage him to make the first move?

He had never been the demon who chased after a guy for sex. He didn't enjoy being the aggressor. Being a demon, many made the wrong assumption about him. Would Fate have given him…

"Do you like honey in your tea?" George asked, breaking Scott out of his head.

Having come to a stop in a large, open-plan living space, Scott noticed how a cluttered counter split the room in two. The word 'den' suited the room. Pillows, cushions, and fleecy looking throws covered the furniture that was large enough to make sitting in either of his blissful one's forms easy. It looked like a great place to snuggle with a view of the large screen TV on one wall or the windows that overlooked what appeared to be a closed in garden. Homely sprang to mind once more. Scott's childhood home had been sterile. No knick-knacks or trinkets. George had plenty, and though they didn't appear in any kind of order, and Scott itched to make them appear more orderly, he liked the feel of the place. Unexpected.

The sound of George clearing his throat brought Scott's gaze back to the man who was now standing, watching Scott closely. "Tea… do you, erm, want some honey in it?" he asked again.

Could he really be any more moronic? "I don't really want tea right now…"

George took another step closer, reaching out, he took hold of the shirt in Scott's hand. "I'm not a romancing type, I don't have fancy words for you like I'm sure you're used to—"

"I'm not." Scott blushed and apologized. "Sorry, I shouldn't have interrupted, continue." He let go of the shirt and cringed on the inside when George tossed it onto the nearest chair. His demon was tutting dramatically.

"Me and my bear, we…"

Scott couldn't stand it any longer and lunged forward—or it was more his demon—and planted his lips on George's. They both groaned, and Scott couldn't find it in him to be cross with his demon half when George tasted so good. Warm spice heated Scott's blood, making it thrum with life. His blissful one.

Ours.

Scott became lost in the kiss, starving for the affection of his blissful one, his bear.

He groaned and parted his lips in invitation. George clasped him tightly, pulling him closer. Heat, overwhelming heat, coursed through him. Despite their sizes nearly matching, George hooked his hands under Scott's ass and hefted him up with an ease that caused Scott's heart to flutter in his chest. The smell of the forest clung to his skin, and Scott breathed in the earthy scent, his cock bucking hard.

Huge hands held onto his ass, and Scott—maybe his demon—removed his clothes with a thought. Then Scott was groaning at the feel of rough finger pads touching him.

"So soft, yet firm." George squeezed his ass as if to make his point, but not hard enough to hurt. "Seems as you're naked and we're... like this... I-I want you. Want to claim you," George murmured against his mouth, not letting up with the kissing. "Is that okay?"

Worry came through, and Scott did his best to drag his thoughts up from another part of his anatomy. If he could get his brain to work and his lips to form words, he'd answer. George gazed at him, clearly seeking an answer, and Scott was back to blushing furiously. His brain was on the fritz! "Please," he croaked out.

Scott's whole body lit up like a damn torch when George didn't put him down, but instead carried him out of the room. His demon was so damn excited he was dancing about doing a booty wiggle.

Honestly, stop, you're putting me off.

As if, he scoffed back, but he did stop, thankfully. His presence remained, and Scott accepted his demon side wanted this as much as Scott did, even if he struggled to say it.

He was on fire. There was no part of him left untouched. Even his cock got a sensual massage thanks to the muscled abdomen it had gotten trapped against.

Even his curling toes felt it. Before they crested the stairs, Scott was embarrassingly close to coming. The beard, silkier than he had considered it would be, rubbed at his skin, warming it and making it tingle as George moved through a doorway. Scott had no chance to look around as his back was placed on a mountain of softness, and George caged him, his mouth pressing against Scott's as his body pushed Scott into the mattress. Tongues stoked together, the tickle of the beard added something to the kiss, and Scott whimpered with how good it felt. The plump lips moved and glided like they were dancing with him. George changed the angle of the kiss and sucked gently on Scott's tongue. The tug traveled straight to his aching shaft. It throbbed as he ground up against solid muscle. The silky texture of skin sliding against his spread the fires through him until his body was alight.

Unsure which way was up, his hips cantered forward, rocking, seeking more friction. His demon half whimpered with how much they wanted to come.

Not me!

"What do you like?" George's growly rumbled words made Scott nearly shoot his load. He whimpered once again, at a loss for an answer.

"Anything," he managed to say past the dryness in his mouth when George looked at him like he could feast on him for days.

Let's hope so.

You're ruining it.

"So pretty," George murmured gruffly, rolling off to the side so he could trail fingers down the exposed flesh to his cock. He rubbed the sticky tip, and Scott groaned, his eyelids fluttering to match his trembling insides.

His bear shimmied down the bed and, in a move that left Scott speechless, deep-throated his cock. He wasn't small, fuck no, but his blissful one had his nose buried in Scott's groin, sucking, slurping so good Scott's balls tightened and throbbed in delight.

Scott let his legs fall apart and George took full advantage as wet fingers slid under Scott's balls. He groaned anew, struggling to drag in a breath at the light touch to his taint, then down to his hole. Slick fingers touched the rim, pressing, circling in a maddening slow tease until he was ready to blow and beg. "I'm gonna come," he confessed, too far gone to be embarrassed by his confession, when it was all he wanted.

George sucked harder, and a finger breached his ass. The added sensation of the intrusion was too much, and his brain shut down as cum hit the back of George's throat.

His groans sent vibrations straight to Scott's clenching ass as he rode the best high of his life.

Drenched in sweat and spent, he then moaned in limp delight at the tongue cleaning his flaccid cock and the continued glide of George's thick digit in and out of his ass.

Slowly finger fucking him, George used his magical tongue to bring his cock back to life. He was fully hard by the time George appeared satisfied with the tonguing he'd given him while stretching his ass.

Feeling empty and aroused, Scott wanted nothing more than to climb on top of his blissful one and…

Don't be selfish!

"Do you want me t-to... y-you know?" Scott stammered and blushed as George came up the bed, flushed with cum on his beard and still wearing his trousers and boots on the bed!

To the demon gods!

George stroked his beard, removing the smear of cum, his big, beautiful eyes watching him closely. "What do you want?"

Scott hardly had control of himself, never mind his demon, at such a question. His demon pushed. "To ride you," he murmured past the tightness of his throat, his demon envisioning the bear's teeth sinking into their flesh and them reciprocating with that juicy, fat cock in their ass that outlined his blissful one's trousers.

George got off the bed, and Scott didn't look away as he stripped. It was hard not to get up and pick up what George had dropped, but the second he kneeled on the bed, nothing else mattered. He nudged Scott over and lay down on his back. The bed Scott noticed was big enough to hold them both easily. "Is this how you see me?"

"Yes," he whimpered. This was like nothing he had experienced, and his demon's eagerness was catching.

George opened his arms wide, and Scott eagerly rolled into them, he had barely touched George before he took hold of his hips and lifted him effortlessly to swing him over the glorious cock waving in the air beneath him.

The head of his cock rubbed pre-cum against his hole where the lube George had used to stretch him remained. The pressure of the wide head breaching him made everything narrow down to his blissful one. Powerful arms bulged under Scott's weight, and a fine layer of sweat made his bear's skin glow. His features were taut with the effort and the time he gave Scott to adjust to the huge cock splitting him in half in the best possible way.

His cock dripped onto George with every inch that slid into him. When Scott's knees touched the covers, he was gasping for breath and ready to blow his load once more.

Work roughened fingers stroked up his sides once Scott settled atop George, their gazes locked. The scent of sex thickened the air in the room. A long moan escaped when George rose up, shifting the cock in his ass.

"Fuck, you're so big."

A smile more wicked than before creased the bear's cheeks. "I'm thinking just the right size for my mate."

Scott shuddered at the possessive tone. He clenched his ass and ground down until it tore a moan from George. He came closer, his hot breath on Scott's throat, so he tilted his head back in offering, moving his hips in a slow roll.

At the feel of teeth grazing the base of his neck, Scott shivered, pushing closer.

"Mine," George uttered against his flesh. Teeth sank in deep, and Scott's whole body locked tight. His ass clenched down so hard he was sure that he'd have an imprint of his blissful one's cock permanently inside him.

His eyelids fluttered closed at the spiraling tendrils of desire he became embraced by. They stroked his skin, flowing freely through him, over him. His heart raced to catch up when George slipped a hand between them, taking hold of his cock and stroking his shaft firmly. His wrist twisted the head, and Scott's balls ached with the need to come.

George sucked on his neck, drinking his blood, and Scott lost his goddamn mind. They now belonged to each other. Never had he hoped to make such a connection after being shunned by many, but his heart now belonged to his honey bear. As the thought registered, cum splattered George's upper body. Scott didn't see it, but there was no way the man crowding him could escape when Scott's demon was moaning like a ten-dollar hooker at the sight of their blissful one covered in their cum. The thick scent of sex hung between them.

The teeth had barely left his skin before Scott and his demon half were reaching up to clasp George's shoulders.

"Our turn," his demon said before Scott could utter a word. It wasn't their way, a touch was all that was needed to form the bond. Right in that moment, it meant nothing when they wanted their blissful one to wear their mark.

George exposed his throat. "Bite me," he demanded in a throaty growl.

Scott's cock gave made a valiant attempt to give more to his blissful one while he struck true. Blood filled his mouth, and he groaned low and needy in his throat as he swallowed, and he felt the cock in his ass thicken, making it hard to move, as cum pulsed deep in his ass.

I've been claimed by my blissful one!

His demon lay back and fanned himself. *Why yes, we have. When can we do that again?*

Chapter Eight

George

It didn't take my mate long to revert to his default settings the demon side warned about. Sitting across from him at his small kitchen table, George could see Scott's fingers were already twitching as if he wanted to straighten out George's things. There had been one brief moment when the two men first woke up, where Scott's hair was mussed in the most delicious fashion, and he was squirming in George's arms trying to almost disappear under his skin as they'd kissed and rocked together, where George felt in tune with his mate.

But the moment they'd climaxed, and George murmured something about breakfast, it was like someone had flipped a switch. The officious Scott, who George had first seen at the hospital, was back, and so were George's insecurities that had him fleeing the hospital in the first place.

Now, dressed in another smart suit that reinforced George's belief that demons could be clothed with a snap of their fingers in either form, his hair immaculate, his phone on the table beside his now empty plate, and a laptop open, it was as if Scott had built a wall between himself and the comfortable messiness of George's home and even George himself.

We need to address this now. Our mate's not comfortable in our space. George's bear didn't understand why, and George could feel the hint of sadness in his bear's concerns. George had set up his house as his safe space, one where he was the most comfortable. Just as he was trying to think how to broach the subject, Scott broke their silence first.

"I failed you yesterday."

George double blinked. "You came to find me in the forest. How was that a failure? Are you regretting your decision?"

There was a pause, and then Scott shook his head. "Not at all," he said quietly. "Back at the hospital, you asked me to help you find out about the paramedic who drugged you, preventing your shift. I was… unsuccessful." He was looking down at his laptop keys as if they held the answer to life.

"I can find out in other ways. Request to see my records, something like that." To be honest, George had forgotten he'd even asked Scott in the first place. "It was probably wrong of me to ask you." *Especially considering I was just making excuses for you to leave.* "Don't worry about it."

"But I do." The concern in Scott's eyes struck George as his mate looked up at him. "You seemed genuinely worried that someone was out to get you. It's my job…" Scott snapped his mouth shut and shook his head. "Sorry. My demon reminded me that bears are very protective and don't like to be perceived as weak or needing to be looked after. What I meant to say is that as you are my blissful one, I'm concerned if you have people after you. Can you tell me more about it?"

"Perceived as weak? Is that what you think of me?" George pinched the top of his nose and then rubbed between his eyes as he wrestled any inappropriate response he didn't want to fire back. "I… I have a family… not that I ever have anything to do with them anymore. But I have a family who think… who thought… Damn it all to hell, I don't like sharing something like this."

"Understood. Fine." The tone suggested Scott was anything but fine, and George winced as he caught the pain his words caused through their bond. Scott tapped his laptop. "Just answer me this, then, my blissful one. Why is there no reference to George Maybank anywhere online? Who are you really?"

Shit. "I paid a lot of money for all references to George Maybank to be wiped from companies that hold their data online," George said stiffly. "I am George Maybank. I legally changed my name about ten years ago, just before I moved here. My original name is unimportant, but suffice to say…" George sighed.

How the hell do I put this?

"Do you remember that spunk of mine you licked off your lovely lips this morning?" Scott's cheeks became slashed with pink, and his nod was jerky. "If you'd slapped that into a jar instead, it wouldn't take you long to find a buyer for it. You've clearly got the skills on the web."

George watched as a myriad of emotions flashed over Scott's face. The wide eyes, the frown, the confusion, and then, just as fast, his professional expression was back. "Are you someone important, from a genetic standpoint?"

"Not in my opinion, no. I'm just a regular bear, making a living as a taxi driver—a job I like because my passengers don't care if I'm surly. I can work my own hours, and there's no dress code. So long as my bits remain covered, no one complains."

"Then why...?" Scott tilted his head slightly, his eyes glazing over, and then he frowned. "Who put a value on your spunk?"

George chuckled, tickled by the possessiveness of his demon. "Your pretty blue demon clearly doesn't like the idea. Is he reading you the riot act?"

The blush was back, but Scott's jaw was tight. "Neither one of us enjoys the idea that someone wants your juices for nefarious purposes. You consider me your mate. Don't I have a right to know what's going on?"

Scott was right, and George didn't need the nudge he got from his bear. Pushing his chair back, George collected their empty mugs and went over to the coffee pot. "My father's considered important in some circles," he said slowly, focusing on getting coffee into the mugs. "Growing up, there were certain behaviors I was expected to participate in, which I didn't because I believed them to be immoral, indecent, and unnecessarily cruel." George closed his eyes as memories flooded his mind. "My beliefs were not well received," he said, determined his sweet little blue demon didn't need all the details.

"People hurt you? They physically punished you? Your family did this to you?"

George focused on counting sugars as he spooned them into his mug. Clearly his mate could get impressions through their bond the same as he could, and while Scott's growl was cute, it wasn't necessary. "After it was determined I wasn't going to live the way my father expected, he decided I was to copulate with others in the clan, with the sole purpose of spreading my genetics. My father's idea was that as I wasn't up to his standards, behavior-wise, he would raise my son in his image instead. He didn't take my refusal well."

Picking up the mugs carefully, George took them back over to the table. "It's become a matter of principle for him. For all I know, my father has since had another son of his own and has completely given up on harvesting my spunk. I don't know. What I know is that I should never have been drugged at the accident site. There was no way I should've been put in a hospital and just left there. Call me a conspiracy theorist if you must, but I've been watching over my shoulder for years, and for good reason. Nothing that happened immediately after the accident makes sense."

"I'll get that information about the paramedic for you." Scott nodded, and George noticed his fingers were twitching again. "I think you'd be safer at my house in the meantime, don't you? Just in case someone tracks you from the hospital to here. I have the best security measures money can buy. You'll be completely safe there."

"I'm not sure I would fit in your place, sweetie." The 'sweetie' he added to try and soften his words, but George looked at Scott's smart suit with its sharp creases and not a stain in sight and then down at the raggy, but very comfortable, sweatpants he'd thrown on to maintain some modesty while they were eating. "I'm not exactly tidy."

"It won't matter." Scott was apparently determined. "George, they drugged you. That could happen again. No one will find you at my place. I need you to be safe."

Scratching the back of his neck, George nodded, even though his gut was screaming at him it was a bad idea. "I can join you there later if you like," he said. "I've got to hunt out the papers for my insurance for my cab, organize a replacement vehicle, and things like that. Were there things you needed to do at the office today, or…" he trailed off. It's not like he knew what Scott did all day, apart from looking like a wet dream walking in his suit.

"I'll get my place ready and stop off at work and finish up a few things there." Scott's smile made George's discomfort worth it. "I can even get some cushions to make it comfortable for you."

"Don't change anything on my account, sweetie." *This is going to be a disaster.*

Chapter Nine

Scott

Leaving George… was *difficult* when he worried for his safety after what he had revealed. The problem was, to do the research he wanted, he needed his blissful one's real name. He chewed over this dilemma to distract him from the ache under his breastbone that came with his departure.

You don't need to work, his demon huffed for the fifth time.

I do! I made a commitment to Dakata.

He left and is flouncing around the forest with his blissful one, he doesn't care.

Flouncing! Dakata hasn't flounced a day in his life. And he has to be in the forest with Silas because Silas does not cope well being away from his tree, as you well know.

Whatever! Our bear needs us to protect him.

You weren't saying that when you thought I was insulting his bearhood! Now, can you give me a minute's peace so I can work to figure out my next steps?

Thankfully, the loud snort was followed by silence as Scott tapped at the laptop on his knee. He answered the endless supply of e-mails that came with his job fast and efficiently.

When the car pulled up outside of Dakata's building, Scott realized he'd promised to get pillows for his apartment to make it more comfortable for George.

We need more than pillows to make your apartment seem less like a doctor's sterile waiting room.

Excuse me! Our apartment is beautiful.

Maybe, but it's not as cozy as our bear's home. That big fur throw rubbing against my skin…

The damn fanning demon was back. *How did I end up with you?*

Lucky, I guess. Anyway. We need lots of similar things to what George has.

Scott wanted to argue, only that would be useless when he wanted George to feel at home in his place. He ran through everything he had seen at George's home. Pulling up one of the main superstores, he started adding stuff to his basket.

Lost in what he was doing, he never considered where he was or that he hadn't bothered to get out of the car until the driver interrupted him.

"Sir, we're here."

"Yes. Thank you." Blushing, he finished what he was doing. Paying for what was in his cart after adding his address and paying extra for same day delivery. He then sent an email to the concierge of his apartment block to advise to expect the delivery, only then did he close his laptop and put it away.

He nodded his thanks and exited the car, going into the building, his thoughts switched to work. Up on the top floor, he'd barely set his bag down on his desk when Luka, Dakata's brother, who had also recently started working for Dakata, appeared. As tall and wide as Dakata, his dark hair was cut short, accentuating a strong jawline. He was attractive, but in a more understated way than his brothers and sister.

"Have you seen Christa?" he asked without preamble, tugging at the black silk tie he wore with his crisp, white shirt, the sleeves rolled up to his elbows, revealing tattoos.

Scott glanced at the office door that Luka had just come out of. "She's not here?" He checked his watch and ran through what appointments she had for the day in his head. "She has nothing in her diary until two pm." Christa, though flighty at times, was usually at work by now.

"No, she skipped out of an important meeting last evening. I've tried calling her but all I'm getting is her voice messaging system. When did you last see her?"

Scott hesitated, recalling Christa's behavior when they had gone to the forest. "She came with me yesterday to the forest—"

"What, Christa willingly went into a forest? Why? Is she with Dakata?"

The questions were fired at Scott without Luka giving him a chance to answer.

"Did they have a planned meeting about the latest band we've signed? Or was it about the venue issues we're having in Paris?"

He continued on, so Scott ran through his own list of things that he needed to do while waiting out Luka.

"Are you listening to me?" Luka snapped, his demon flaring in his eyes.

"Christa willingly went into the forest. I don't know why. No, she was not with Dakata, that I am aware of. Dakata has agreed to the terms for the new signing, and I have sent the contracts out. Paris, Merihem, is dealing with." He met Luka's gaze, unfazed. "I think that was everything. Now, if you don't mind, I have a list of my own to get through."

Luka looked him up and down, frowning. "There's something different about you." His nose wrinkled as he stepped closer. "You smell different." His eyes widened when they dropped to the collar of his shirt.

"I have a blissful one." His demon danced around at how those words sounded.

Luka gasped, running a hand through his hair. "You, too." He looked around like someone might jump on him any second. "Fuck, it's like a contagion. Spreading!"

He took a step back from Scott, who rolled his eyes.

"Yes, well, it's a wonderful thing to find the other half of your soul," he murmured, recalling how gorgeous his bear looked naked, sweaty, and covered in cum after they had claimed each other. There was no feeling like it in the world. The connection he'd never felt with his family, he had discovered with George. A family who would quickly find out that Scott had a blissful one with how demons gossiped.

He would need to ring them, and that filled him with dread at what they might want. Luka, moving further away from him, snapped Scott out of his thoughts.

Back were the wide eyes. "Whatever, I just need to speak to Christa. If she turns up, tell her it's urgent." On that he stalked off, heading down the corridor to where he had an office, only once looking back with a strange expression Scott didn't bother to try to interpret. His mind had already shifted gears back to George and the need to find out who the paramedic was.

He sat at his desk and made a point of checking that he'd dealt with all of his work-related things first because he took his job seriously. George would get that, right?

Our bear will have other things to worry about, like how anal retentive you are over everything being in the right place, his demon said sarcastically.

Scott took a deep breath, counted to ten, then replied, *order is not a bad thing!*

He opened up a search bar on his computer and made a purposeful effort to block his demon. He had some contacts, because of his family, in shady places, Scott had no call to use them before. For George, he would cross the line he'd drawn when he'd left the demon realm.

Two calls, and he had the information he needed on the paramedic and could search to see if he had any worrying connections to shifters who dealt in sperm. An hour later, Scott sat back, frowning at the screen. From his searches, the paramedic didn't appear to have anything to hide. He'd been on the job for three weeks and had trained for the last three years to be able to deliver emergency care.

Staring at the screen at the innocuous human, Scott had two options: believe everything he had found or go and find the guy and *question him in person*. By his family's standard, that meant intimidation and threats to glean the truth.

That wasn't something Scott had ever done, but for his blissful one, he was willing to change that if it meant protecting him from his father. He didn't sigh, though it was a close call when he thought about how George wasn't really George, and he didn't trust Scott with the truth.

If he dwelled too hard on that, he knew he would spiral back into past behaviors of believing he wasn't good enough, and with that came the crushing urge to control everything in his vicinity. He'd already seen how George reacted to his fastidiousness.

He shut down his computer, checked the time, went into Christa's office to leave her a message, then collected his laptop and headed for the door.

Back in the car minutes later, he gave the paramedics' address to the driver. He wasn't sure if he was going off on a wild goose chase, but Scott needed to know why the fool had injected George to prevent him from shifting. If he needed to scare him to find out, then so be it.

He fiddled with his laptop, checking things to distract him when his cell phone rang. One look at the screen and he cursed. How the hell had they found out so fast?

"Hello, Mother," he murmured, accepting the call, expecting some hysteria.

"Don't you 'hello mother' me, I've heard nothing from you for weeks. Your brother's birthday dinner arrangements were emailed to you two weeks ago, and I've had no response as to whether you will attend alone."

There was no question of him not attending, despite whether Scott had other plans, but that was his family. That she hadn't mentioned George had to mean Luka had not spilled the beans to anyone yet. Demons were notoriously bad for keeping anything to themselves.

Was this the perfect opportunity for George to meet all his family? He shuddered at the thought, but he'd never attend a family function and not take his blissful one. Someone he was proud to be with. Giving George the impression he might somehow be embarrassed to be seen with him would never do. "I work a lot of hours, Mother. Being responsible about my job takes priority over dinner arrangements, regardless of what it's for." He knew even saying it would make no odds, but he continued to try.

"So, you're coming alone, *again.*"

"No, I will have a plus one—"

"Miracles will never cease. Good, it will even up the table arrangement. Don't be late." She was gone before he could respond.

He groaned and considered sending a message to explain who George was to him, then decided against it. In-person was always best with his family. Always.

The car slowed, and he stowed his phone and computer. "We're here, sir."

Scott placed his laptop bag down. "Can you please wait? I won't be long." Or he hoped he wouldn't be, especially with how his demon gave a devilish laugh, cracking his knuckles.

Chapter Ten

George

Grimacing, George pulled his new taxi into a public parking space outside of Scott's building. He was torn. George knew the place. He'd poured many rich idiots out of his cab and onto the curb on any night ending in Y. People with more money than sense who spoke in their lofty tones about shit that clearly sounded great in their drunken heads, but definitely didn't translate well when the words came out.

If George had any choice in the situation, he wouldn't set foot in the foyer, let alone in one of the apartments. Or rather, the penthouse apartment, because Scott had texted him his address and said he would be home about four.

It was a quarter past four. Thinking about it, George felt as though it had been the longest day of his damn life. Being apart from his demon, even after just one night, was hell on earth, making George wonder how he was going to work. It's not like he could park Scott in the back of his cab as he did his job, but he doubted he would be a lot of use curled up in a corner of Scott's office, either.

His bear had been no help—alternating between sulking when George's fare had him driving away from Dakata's office and getting all hyped up if they were heading in that direction. George told his bear countless times they did not know if Scott was even there... but it didn't make any difference.

Suck it up, George warned his inner worry wart. The one thing that consoled George over the very long day was that he'd heard demons didn't have the same sense of attachments to mates/blissful ones that shifters did, so Scott wouldn't be feeling any discomfort.

Admittedly, Dakata was pretty much tied to Silas every minute of every day, but that was because Silas had such a deep bond with his tree and the forest. George was sure Merihem had gone to Dakata's office on his own, without Peni sometimes. Dougal had told him about how Peni had been attacked at Dakata's house while Merihem wasn't there. So, it was possible to be separated from a blissful one, even if it wasn't often. It was enough to prove, in George's mind at least, that demons didn't have that same need to be with their blissful ones that George's bear seemed to have to be with his mate.

A need that meant he had to brave the foyer of the apartment complex from hell.

Getting out of his car, George locked it, trying to ignore how the vast apartment complex loomed above him as he got closer. Built in chrome, steel, and glass, it stood proudly above the skyline as a giant 'fuck you' to the more modest buildings around it. There were no trees or gardens, not a whiff of greenery. Just two white marble statues depicting ancient gods flanking the wide concrete path leading to the main entrance.

George shuddered as he got closer. *Like living in a glass coffin,* he thought glumly, even as his steps quickened when his bear anticipated seeing their mate.

Pushing open the large door, glass, of course, George nodded at a man standing beside a reception counter, making his way to the elevator.

"I say. You there." George turned to address the man calling out to him. "I don't know where you're going, but you can't just wander in here as if you own the place."

"I'm heading up to the penthouse suite." George pointed in the air with his middle finger. If the concierge got the wrong idea about his action, that was on him. "I've been invited, and I'm expected."

"That demon on the top floor doesn't have visitors. More importantly, he hasn't informed *me* he's expecting visitors," the concierge said in that snooty tone that made George's teeth clench. "It's bad enough I've spent half the day arranging carriage for his numerous parcels. He insisted on them being delivered today when he knows the delivery day is Friday. Frankly, sir, piss off. I'm not losing my job because you got it into your fool head to go annoying people who protect their privacy like it's gold."

Stalking closer, his fists clenched, George kept his voice low. "You have a phone right there on your desk. A man who was good at his job would be picking up that handset and speak to the occupant in the penthouse suite, informing him that George Maybank is in reception. I'm not the type to cost you your job, as you seem to think I am, but..." he reached into his pocket and pulled out his own phone. "If I call the occupier of the penthouse suite and let him know someone at the front desk is preventing me from going up to see him…" he trailed off expectantly. Most men in that position would at least consider his suggestion.

The concierge was clearly built from stubborn stock and shook his head vehemently. "That demon has lived up there since this place was built. He does not have visitors. I have had no notification from him that he's expecting company this afternoon or any afternoon. For the last time, leave these premises, or I will call security."

There was a thread of fear behind the strong words. George could smell it, and that wasn't an unusual reaction seeing as George was probably twice his size. The problem was the concierge was standing firm, and in his own weird way, George respected that. "I'll make my call outside," he said, saluting the man with his phone as he went back out the door he'd just come through again.

Tapping Scott's contact number, the phone barely rang once before Scott answered. He sounded breathless and his voice poured out of the phone speaker in a rush. "George? Where are you, George? Have you been taken again? Do you need me to save you?"

George chuckled. "No, I've not been taken again. I didn't get taken the first time, remember? I'm…"

"Well, why aren't you here? I have all this stuff, cushions, and things, so you'll feel comfortable in my space, but I don't know what you like. I don't know how to arrange the things, so they look right. There're boxes and packaging all over my floor..."

"Scott. Scott!" His poor demon seemed to be having a meltdown. "Look out of your window. Look down to the public parking lot." George stepped out of the awning of the building entrance, moving far enough away from the building so he could see the windows of the penthouse suite. "Are you looking out of the window? Can you see me?"

"I can see you. Thank goodness. I can see you. Why are you down there? I need you up here. I ordered all these things, and they arrived, and now I don't know where to put anything, and my space is all so messy..."

"Scott, honey. When you arranged for the delivery of everything you bought to help me feel comfortable in your space, did you tell your man at the door I was coming? Only..."

"He won't let you in? Oh, no, no, no..." Scott groaned loudly. "I ordered the stuff, and then I had work to do, and then I went to see the paramedic, and I... I... don't go anywhere. I'm coming. I'm coming, George. Oh, no, oh, no, oh, no..."

There was a loud clatter—the sort of noise George equated with an anxious demon dropping his phone and running out of the room. He moved back so he was under the awning, and waved at the concierge who glared at him through the glass.

Seconds later, and it genuinely could only have been the length of time it took for Scott to come down the elevator, Scott came running into the foyer, yelling, "You ass, you're fired. You should've picked up the damn phone," pointing at the concierge as he kept running to the door.

"George. Oh, George." Scott was puffing as he opened the door, causing it to slam into the wall with a loud bang. His face was red, and his hair was definitely askew, a sight that warmed George's heart. "Come in. Come in. I'm so sorry. I was so busy organizing everything else. This man is my blissful one, you asshole," he yelled at the shocked-looking concierge. "Do you know how rare they are and how amazing it is that I have one?"

"He was protecting your privacy, Scott," George said gently, not at all surprised that Scott was in a position to fire the concierge. Demons preferred to own and control their environments, and it made sense that Scott would own the building, now he thought about it. "That's what you pay him for. You can't fire him for doing his job."

"I can." Scott pouted rather dramatically. "I absolutely can if I want to."

"But you don't want to. This gentleman and I have met now. He knows I'm allowed in the building, so there won't be any trouble from now on, will there?" George quirked his eyebrow at the man, who was visibly shaking.

"No, Mr. Maybank." The man shook his head so fast, George worried his hair would fly off. "I didn't know. I know now. It won't happen again."

"See?" George said at the still pouting Scott, which was adorable because those dimples seemed to dance in the sharp planes of his cheeks. "He won't do it again. So we can go up now and work on straightening your space, so you feel comfortable in it."

"I bought so much stuff," Scott mumbled, but he let George lead him away. "I really wanted you to be comfortable, and my demon said my space is sterile. So, I clicked and clicked, and it never seems like a lot when it's in a cart online, but then it arrives, and there were just boxes and boxes..."

"Hey, hey, hey." George waited until the elevator door closed before pulling Scott into his arms, inhaling his mate's unique scent, settling both him and his bear. "I did say you didn't have to do anything. I understand you like all your items arranged in their correct spaces."

"I can't help that I do." Scott seemed to cling on for a second until the elevator door dinged, indicating they'd arrived. "But look at all this *mess*."

George put his arm across the elevator door to stop it from closing. "Scott, hon, you do realize this is the hallway." There were a lot of boxes, some empty, a few half open, and the rest still taped up. "Were you planning to unpack it all out here and then move it into your apartment?"

"My apartment's already *full*." Scott grabbed his hand and hurried him down the hallway, dodging boxes and even kicking one that got in his way.

He tapped a few numbers into a small box on the side of the single doorway George could see and flung open the door. "Just look at it all."

At first glance, George couldn't see anything wrong with the space at all. It was a wide open-plan room. There was a solitary couch, in white, that stood out in stark contrast to the dark wooden floors. A single television screen was the only thing adorning the white walls. The penthouse had enormous windows, which let in a lot of light and a gorgeous view of the setting sun. Beyond the "living area," and George used that term loosely, he could see pure white cupboards in the kitchen area, and countertops that shone despite being black granite.

What am I missing? George looked around, especially around the couch area. He noticed three bright cushions, one yellow, one red and one blue, put in a neat pile by the side of the couch, which was why he missed it before, and there was also a rug. It wasn't big, but it was similar in color to the one George had in his own house.

"There's a lot of room on the floor," he offered, not sure what Scott was getting upset about. "Were you short of cupboard space or bookshelves?"

"I've got bookshelves." Running across to the wall, Scott pressed on a panel under the television, revealing a hidden cubby hole that was lined with shelves. They were stacked full of colorful cushions and soft throw rugs. "They're full up. I've still got to find space for all the stuff in the hallway."

George bit his lip, trying so hard not to laugh at the meltdown. "What about in the bedroom? Cushions are nice on the bed."

"I've done that, too." Scott disappeared down a hallway to the side of the kitchen. "Come and see."

Following the cute butt down the hallway, George could see the room before Scott walked into it. Again, it had wide, high windows, the same dark wood floor, and an enormous bed that took up most of the space. It was covered in a white bedspread. Perched up were pillows, four of them wrapped in white pillow slips. There were another two pillows, round ones. Both were yellow, and neither one of them was much bigger than George's palm.

"I don't have room for anything else." Going over to the bed, Scott picked up one of the pillows and moved it about an inch closer to the other one. Then he stood back, frowning. A moment later, he went around to the other side of the bed and moved the other cushion an inch closer to the one he'd just moved. But it was clear he still wasn't happy with the arrangement.

"Scott, hon, leave the cushions alone." George went around the bed, pulling his mate into his arms. "I'm happy you tried to make me comfortable, but you don't like these things, and that's not the way mating works."

"But I have all those boxes, and I've still got to take out the trash, and…" Scott was clearly overwhelmed.

"Go and fix your hair and your face," George suggested. "Change your clothes into something more comfortable. While you're doing that, I'll break down the empty boxes and tape up the other ones that are still full, if you've got any tape. You can return all the items we're not going to use. All right?"

"I just want you to be safe and comfortable." Scott slumped against him.

"I know, hon." George gave Scott an extra squeeze. "I'll tidy up the hallway, and you can tidy yourself. Then we'll go out for a meal, I got my new cab today. We won't be going anywhere fancy, just burgers from a food cart, so you don't need to dress up. And when we've eaten, and you've relaxed a bit, you can tell me what you found out about the paramedic you investigated for me."

"There was nothing to find. I went and talked to him personally to make sure," Scott said, sounding glum. "The paramedic was just following what he'd been taught to do. He'd only been on the job three weeks, and the department had a meeting just two days ago saying all shifters needed to be medicated if they were injured and traveling in an ambulance for the safety of the driver and staff."

That doesn't explain how the paramedic knew I was a shifter in the first place, but George didn't see the point in pushing his overwhelmed mate into finding out anything else. He could do that himself in his own time. "Well, let's go and get some burgers. I think you need a chance to get out of the apartment for a while and destress."

"We can't do that either." Scott's frown deepened. "The boxes are going to have to wait, and you're going to need a suit." He clicked his fingers and suddenly George was wearing a very smart, and definitely not him, tuxedo. "My mom called. We're expected there for dinner tonight. It's my brother's birthday."

"Where's there?" George had a sinking feeling in his gut. "Do they live locally?"

"No, they live in the demon realm." Scott ran his hands through his hair, and suddenly he was wearing a tuxedo that matched George's, and his hair was immaculate again. "It's a family event. That makes it a perfect time to introduce my blissful one to the whole family all at the same time, don't you think?"

"If you say so, hon." George wasn't sure who was trying to convince who.

Chapter Eleven

Scott

What did George mean by *'If you say so, hon'*? Did he sound unconvinced about the meeting with his family? Was he passing along his own nerves about such an occasion?

"You do know I want you to meet my family? If you are picking up I'm nervous… it's just… they can be a little… stuffy." That word did not cover just how snobby his family was. Oh, to the demon gods, what was he playing at? This was going to be a disaster.

The meltdown over the things he'd bought and couldn't quite figure out their placement didn't appear to have fazed his bear, which was good. His demon was laughing its damn ass off over the pillow placements. Scott really couldn't see what was so funny!

Now he was having another meltdown, like some kind of drama llama, only in demon form. What was George to think of him?

Large hands cupped his cheeks, and then all that he could do was feel. Heat and passion from George's kiss didn't allow anything else to filter past. He moaned low in his throat, and it rumbled out when George let go.

His gaze held Scott's. "It's gonna be alright. We go, we eat, you introduce me, then we leave."

Was it really that simple? Scott had no evidence to suggest anything with his family was that simple, he just didn't want to contradict his blissful one.

He reached for George's hand and intertwined their fingers. "Let's believe that." He took a deep, George-scented breath, filling his lungs, and focused on what was important. "Have you ever translocated before?"

George gave him an intrigued look. "Nah, that's not part of a shifter's skill set."

Squeezing the fingers, offering reassurance. "I tend not to do it often, but it's the only way for us both to get to the demon realm. So just hold on to me, and maybe shut your eyes. Some have said the first time can be a little disorientating."

"Good to know," he muttered, shutting his eyes, looking sexy, though Scott had to agree with his demon, they much preferred their bear out of formal clothes—as in naked.

He took another breath and focused on where he wanted to go and a moment later, he was in his parent's home, in his old bedroom, holding the gift he'd bought for his brother months ago.

"Is it safe to open my eyes?" George questioned.

Scott glanced around the dusty, box-ridden bedroom that his family used to store their junk in. That spoke volumes about how they thought of him. His brothers' rooms remained maintained for visits. "Yes," he replied in a neutral tone. One that he'd become forced to use while in this house.

"Hardly felt a thing. A little zappy feeling over my body, but nothing bad. My bear wants to know can we do that to the forest if he's in a rush?" A cheeky grin added to George's attractiveness and gave Scott a little boost his demon was all for.

"We can do whatever your bear wants," answered his demon side before Scott could form his own reply.

I would have said yes.

I was just making sure of it.

Scott resisted rolling his eyes at his demon, not wanting George to get the wrong impression.

"Your demon side has a very sexy voice."

See, I'm his favorite.

He can't have favorite's, you idiot, as we are basically one.

I'm not anal retentive, and I take offense at you suggesting I would ever be like you! He shuddered hard enough that Scott had to hold on to the parcel in his hand.

"Please don't encourage him," Scott begged, keeping hold of George's hand to head to the door, realizing the argument could continue for some time and then he'd get chastised for being late by his mother. Something he did not wish to subject his blissful one to, when she could resemble a harpy. "He's bad enough without believing you favor him over me."

George pulled Scott to a halt before he could tuck the parcel under his arm and open the door. "You're our mate, it's that simple."

Scott felt his demon's conflict as his cheeks ached from the grin he got, thanks to the sincerity and pride coming from their blissful one. He came forward and kissed him softly. "It is, blissful one."

The door in front of them opened, and Scott's groan was all inside his mind as he reluctantly pulled away, already knowing who was watching them by the scent of his father's cloying aftershave. He glanced sideways. "Father."

"I thought I heard voices. What are you doing in the storeroom?"

His snooty tone made Scott stiffen. "It was once my bedroom, if you recall." He looked at George, working to keep his embarrassment in check. "George, this is my father, Randal."

Father barely allowed his gaze to shift in George's direction, the slight was impossible to ignore.

"Nice to meet you," George said politely, offering his hand.

When his father hesitated, Scott stiffened further, his back aching with tension, and he'd barely been in the house a minute or more. "Father!" he snapped, "George is my blissful one." The latter, he said with great joy.

"What!" The disbelief was easy to read as he finally looked fully at George, mouth agape, eyes bulging out of their sockets.

Scott's demon bristled at the condescending look, and Scott had to work to keep from shifting.

We aren't starting a fight, do you hear me?

How could I not when you're bellowing at me?

Was I?

You are. It's alright, hon.

Oh bugger, he was, and now George had heard him, too. *It's not alright at all. I will not let them treat you the same as they treat me. I won't.*

His parents dressed and preferred to stay in their human form, Scott had no recollection of seeing his father's demon in years. They had the lord of the manner act down to a tee. This was mostly why Scott had so much conflict over the two halves of himself.

The click of heels made Scott's anxiety coil tighter, and he groaned internally at who was coming.

George ran a reassuring hand down his back and brought him closer as Scott's mother appeared in the doorway, wearing a pinched look of disdain as she glanced into the room. "Why are we standing around in the storeroom? Dinner is about to be served. You know I can't abide lateness, Scott. It's so like you to act with no consideration for your family."

She never so much as acknowledged George, further insulting Scott. He had a thick skin, one he had developed over the decades because of their behavior towards him. He had no such thickness when it came to George. "Mother, I'd like to introduce you to George, my blissful one," he gritted out, forcing his lips into a tight smile.

"There's that damn thing again. Blissful one, what nonsense is this? He's clearly not a demon." His father's long, pointy nose wrinkled when he came forward by half an inch—like he might catch something if he stepped closer—and sniffed the air. "He's a bear!"

"He's my bear." The snap to his tone would have flayed skin from bone at the insult no one in a mile radius would miss. "The demon gods blessed me with a blissful one, and all you can say is he's a bear? What happened to *congratulations, son*? Or is that too much to ask?" he asked sarcastically, fighting his demon every inch from shifting.

His anger matched that of his demon, but fighting was never the answer. He'd learned that growing up. Although this time his family had outdone themselves, they hadn't gotten beyond his own bedroom—storeroom—that was a first even for his family before the insults started.

"I'm not sure what's going on here, but Scott's my claimed mate. One I'm proud to have—"

"I'm sure you are being a lowly bear," his mother said haughtily, nose pointing in the air as if seeking cleaner air.

"Lowly bear, how dare you insult my blissful one!" Scott bellowed, and was met with two stunned expressions. In the whole of his life he had worked to please his parents—unsuccessfully, he might add—and now he could see that even the gift the gods had bestowed on him wasn't proof enough that he was worthy of being a part of this family. It hurt, but not as much as George being treated with such disrespect.

When his demon pushed once more, he didn't stand in his way. The gift when flying, then gone was the tuxedo, and his demon stood—naked—in all his pale blue glory. "Acknowledge our blissful one," he bellowed, causing the room to shake and boxes to fall.

The sound of shoes clattering down the hall made not one iota of difference to his demon, Scott was a little more conflicted at his brothers seeing him like this. They'd been merciless about his pale skin when they'd been growing up.

George, it appeared, had enough, not that Scott could blame him. "I think it's time we left." He hooked an arm through theirs, not taking his gaze off the group of demons all vying to get into the room past the two statues he'd reduced his parents to by letting his demon out.

"Not before they acknowledge you," his demon persisted, glancing at George. All he wanted was for them to see how wonderful their bear was. It was that simple.

His family was not that simple.

"The king is going to hear about this!" his father, having finally found his tongue, snapped in a strangled voice, spitting angry darts at George. "We will get this mix-up rectified."

The roar was deafening as his demon lost his shit at the idea that their blissful one was a mix-up. "Mix-up! Mix-up."

George turned his back on those vying for attention and reached up to once more cup their cheeks, holding his gaze. "Take me home, sweetie, I'll take you out for a burger." He flicked a glance over his shoulder, giving his family a pitiful look. "At least then we'll be able to enjoy it without the atmosphere of condescending asshole choking us."

Scott snorted, and his demon found the humor in the situation, laughing heartily at the pointed dart hitting home when silence descended from those in the doorway.

Only it didn't last for long. Scott should have known they wouldn't escape that easily.

"You are aware of who you are speaking to?" His father's tone could freeze a demon's balls right off. While his demon magic held Scott prisoner, unable to translocate.

George, as if sensing the immediate panic running through Scott at what his father might try to do to him, to George, growled, low and mean, swinging around to the sound of tearing clothes.

Chapter Twelve

George

George had one major peeve when it came to dealing with people—those who thought they were somehow special and entitled to insult and belittle those around them without consequence. Scott was being held, he could feel the magic in the air, and the thought that a man would do that to his own son, while his mother and brothers looked on as if they were watching a carnival act, brought back memories George had of dealing with his own father.

His father and Scott's could've been cut from the same cloth—snooty, privileged, and determined that their belief systems were the only way life could and should be lived. George hadn't fought his father—he'd escaped. But back then, the only thing he was trying to save was the right to use his spunk as he saw fit. Now someone who was a damn clone of his own father was threatening his mating.

He didn't even think about the implications of shifting in the demon realm. Put bluntly, George didn't give a shit. Scott's beautiful demon's face became frozen, as if he was a pale blue statue, his mouth open, his eyes caught mid-blink.

The panic running through their bond was like a match to George's anger, and his bear burst through.

He didn't hesitate, even as the scraps of the tuxedo Scott had given him fell like ribbons to the floor. He lunged straight for Randal, clearly catching the demon unawares. His bear's teeth sunk into the demon's leg, the taste of the leathery skin and cologne searing his tongue.

Resisting the urge to spit and longing for a tall glass of water, the bear released his teeth, spinning around and knocking the demon to the floor with his back end. He felt the change, as the man let go of his magical hold on Scott, but the bear wasn't finished.

He wouldn't bite a woman—he wasn't sure his teeth would make it through the clearly fake crystal sheen on her skin in the first place—but he didn't have an issue with knocking her off her six-inch heels, wincing at the sound of her scream.

"Randal. Help me."

"Help yourself, woman. I'm wounded here," Randal screeched like the whining asshole he was.

Meh. It's just a nip. George focused on the brothers, curling his lip over his long teeth, and he stared them down.

"Hey, we were just laughing. We didn't do nothing." The tallest one backed up, his hands raised. "I never thought my little brother would ever be into bestiality, but whatever floats your boat, man."

George lunged, his huge paws landing on the man's chest and bringing him to the ground. The smell of urine wrinkled his nose, but George could feel magic in the air again and didn't linger. The other two brothers were already running down a long and narrow hallway, and George gave chase. He wasn't built for marathon running, but he could move fast over short distances.

The timing was perfect. It was a moment that would become emblazoned in George's memory forever more. One screamed, one yelled, and then a satisfying thud, thud,

thud, as the two demons fell headfirst down the stairs, tumbling head over ass, their limbs hitting the walls on the way down. Yeah, George's bear felt he could afford to swagger a bit.

Except when he turned around, the bear heard Scott yell, "Look out, honey bear," and he saw the flash of a fireball coming toward him.

That's going to singe some fur, he thought as he ducked and dodged, feeling a flash of pain as his cells broke down. Seconds later, they were back in Scott's apartment, and the bear was being smothered by an overly affectionate demon.

"Honey bear, oh, my poor, poor honey bear, you've been *hit*!" George's furry face was being subjected to a thousand demon butterfly kisses. "What can I do? Tell me, honey bear, what can I do to make those ouches go away? They burned your fur, those horrid people. They burned my precious bear."

Oh, no, Scott's demon was crying. The bear tried to turn his head so he could see the extent of the damage. The smell of singed fur was never nice, but the demon had his cheeks gripped firmly.

"They held me with magic and my own father stopped me going to you. You were so brave, trying to protect me and they hurt you, burned your lovely fur." The demon was sobbing harder. "Is it any wonder I try to keep things nice? Did you see what they did to my room? And they threatened to go to the king. I should be the one to go to the king. I should have them thrown into the hell pits for hurting my blissful one… I'm so sorry."

Giving up on trying to see the state of his fur, the bear licked up the demon's tears, and then George came through when that wasn't working. "Hey, hey," he said softly. "It's okay."

"It's not. It's really not." The poor demon was heartbroken. "They make fun of my coloring, they tease me because I'm smaller than they are. They've never once been proud of me for the work I do for Dakata and make fun of me for that, too. Even my room—did you see the state of my room? That's where I grew up. I hated it there, but that room was always nice. We kept it lovely. And now it's messy. A place for them to dump their shit. They attacked you, they hurt you, they called you a mix-up like you were one of those annoyances my father had to fix. I hate them. I hate what they did to you."

"It's not the first time I've met people like that." Using his thumbs, George wiped away more tears. "You've had a rough time of it…"

"Me? What about you?" Scott came through, his hair a mess, his eyes red-rimmed. "I swear… please believe me, I promise if I'd have known they'd be so rude, or cruel, or hurt you… I can't believe my father…" Scott trailed off and sniffed. "I would never have taken you there if I thought you'd be hurt. I'm so very sorry."

"I'm fine. A shift will fix most things for a shifter. Did you want to get dressed and go out for a burger with me?"

"Really? That's all you're going to say? We should, I suppose." Scott was looking around, clearly distracted. "You didn't even get to eat before the insults started. Oh, no…"

George looked over in the direction Scott was looking and saw the neat pile of three cushions by the couch had fallen, so they lay sprawled over the floor.

"I'll just…"

"The burgers can wait," George said firmly, catching Scott before he ran off and pulling him close. His poor mate needed kisses. They both needed kisses, and if a bit of mess got made along the way… well, hopefully, Scott would be too tired to notice.

Chapter Thirteen

Scott

Everything about the evening, or the lack of it, made Scott tumble down into the pit of hell, where he needed everything to go back to being controlled. Orderly.

What was he to do?

He'd cried all over their bear. Then, the sweet honey bear had licked his tears away. He hadn't chastised him. Called him a baby.

The mess…

George's mouth became persistent, and his thoughts melted away. The world shrank down to the gentle kisses that made his chest warm and his belly quiver.

Large hands cupped his ass and lifted him effortlessly. Heat and the wonderful smell of George surrounded him, protected him. Being smaller than those in his family, Scott hated feeling less. In George's arms, he exulted in the knowledge his bear could hold him like this. He moaned at the feel of their naked bodies touching as he wrapped himself around George, clinging on. Safe.

Loved.

His demon side was right. Despite the blissful one connection, there was more to it, and whether they were ready to utter those words aloud, Scott felt cherished for the first time in his existence. It was… *amazing.* Somewhere in the back of his mind, the worry about everything—him—being perfect didn't seem to matter. How long it would last, Scott wasn't sure, but he clung to it now as he did to George.

When his back touched the cool cotton of the comforter on his bed, George didn't stop the gentle exploration of his mouth. Gentle nips were followed with his teasing tongue before he deepened the kiss. A drug of affection, his lips delivered to Scott, stealing away the need to do more than lay there and feel.

Hovering over him, only their mouths touching, Scott's eyes grew heavy along with his limbs. Desire hummed between them, yet it wasn't frantic, more a slow ebb. It washed through him with each kiss that left him in a languid state of arousal.

So different from anything he'd experienced before, Scott was in heaven. His mouth was fully sensitized to that of George's. "Such lovely kisses," he murmured dreamily when George trailed kisses down the side of his neck towards Scott's mate mark, only to nibble on the skin, making his cock jerk and the urgency to run back through his veins chasing away the dreaminess with its fire.

"Like that, do we?"

The rumbled words barely penetrated as George moved lower, his mouth teasing over Scott's collarbone, his tongue and lips tasting.

When he reached Scott's nipple, it was a hard bud begging for touch. George's hot breath teased the bud, and Scott moaned and pushed up, desperate to feel the talented mouth.

"Look how beautiful you are," he rasped and sucked the nipple between his lips. Scott felt the pull all the way to his cock as George's cheeks hollowed.

"Ughh," Scott cried out when George pinched the other bud and rolled it between his fingers. His cock bucked and leaked between his legs untouched, the need an ache deep in his gut.

"That's it. Just focus on me. On what you're feeling."

The place could have been attacked by a horde of raging demons all screaming at the top of their lungs, and Scott wouldn't have noticed when those talented lips sealed once more around his tight bud and sucked. The ache grew inside him and the feelings intensified with each touch, tug, nip, and suck. George had done no more than touch him from lips to nipples. It was madness and delight rolled into one. He didn't want to move despite how desperate he was to come because he never wanted this to end. He'd die a happy demon right here, never moving from this one spot if George kept doing what he was doing.

George's chuckle brushed his skin. "Let's hope there's no dying for some time. I haven't nearly started to explore this delicious body. And I'm more than happy to play with your body."

He clearly had read all of Scott's thoughts and his demon was lying back on a damn couch and once more fanning himself at their blissful one's sentiment.

One, it seemed, he wanted to prove as he moved from nipple to nipple, touching, biting, licking, watching each and every reaction Scott had as he hovered over him, his own cock as hard and aroused as Scott's, yet he didn't rush.

On and on, George treasured Scott until he was a gibbering mess on the verge of coming. "I need to come," he begged, just needing something but unsure of what, he was so out of it.

George's mouth released his nipple, and on all fours, he moved back, trailing kisses down Scott's quivering stomach muscles until it was there by the head of his sticky cock. Scott struggled to open his eyes to watch as George gave him an enticing smile full of wickedness before his lips parted wide, and he swallowed Scott down to the root. Moist heat surrounded his shaft, and then George hallowed his cheeks, sucking.

"Argghhhhhhhh," Scott screamed when his balls pulled tight, and then they off-loaded in a violent torrent of cum down George's willing throat. White clouded his vision before his eyes slammed shut, and his body bowed at the next tug from the deep suction.

He scented George's seed and groaned anew, his balls aching as his cock throbbed, releasing the last of his cum. George's mouth relaxed, and he lapped Scott's cock clean. Soft kitten licks as he finally stretched out at the side of him.

He drifted on the dreaminess for some time before he heard George's stomach growl and gurgle.

Food, they needed food. The problem was Scott's limbs were more liquid than bone from…

The nipple fucking we just got.

What? Scott choked back, feeling his nipples tingle at his demon's accurate description.

We need to get him to do that again.

Stop being so greedy.

Am not.

Are, too.

"You two are cute, but I could do with a burger before I," George lifted his head up to glance up at Scott, a light in his eyes Scott's demon groaned at—the light of promise—"nipple fuck you again."

Scott grabbed one of the pillows on the bed and buried his face in it, hiding his pink cheeks.

The bed shifted, then the pillow got tugged away, and all Scott could scent was his cum on George's breath as he came nose to nose with him. His dark gaze held Scott's. "I'll give you whatever you want, my pretty demon, never worry about that." He kissed him again, and Scott forgot all about being embarrassed. In fact, Scott pretty much forgot about everything.

Two hours later, Scott licked the tomato juice that had leaked out of the burger bun—they had delivered and he'd just finished—off his fingers.

It might have taken another hour to get out of bed after his demon side wanted to appear and get George to play with his nipples, too. Explaining that they were one, and the same had not worked, and George didn't seem to have an issue with it, so Scott was trying not to think too hard about it.

Now that he'd filled his belly, his gaze moved beyond the kitchen counter they sat at. He was no longer distracted, and the worries wanted to take a bite out of his relaxed state.

Don't you even think about cleaning. I mean it.

It has to be done, and you don't enjoy doing it, he argued back.

Who the hell enjoys cleaning?

He went to get up and George lay a hand on his arm, the other held his third burger.

Scott paused and arched a brow, hoping like hell he'd not caught him fighting with his demon about cleaning. That would be mortifying.

"I haven't finished, and I'd much prefer if you stay here with me, if that's alright with you?"

He gave him such a hopeful, gorgeous smile, Scott's bottom remained on the chair, his gaze on his blissful one and thoughts of tidying up forgotten at the lovely request. His chest warmed once more, his heart fluttering. "Of course."

"So, did you have any hobbies?"

"Hobbies?" Scott asked, at a loss.

"Yep." George used his serviette to dab at his lips. "I like to go watch ice hockey when my team are playing local. I don't much care for watching it on the TV, you can't quite get the feel of how rough they get with each other." He winked at Scott, and went back to munching on his burger, his attention though remained on Scott… waiting.

No one had ever asked about his interests before, so it took a second or three to gather his flustered thoughts. "I love to read and go to second-hand bookshops to see what treasures I can find."

"That so. Treasures no less."

Seeing he wasn't joking at Scott's expense, and sounded intrigued by his answer, he grinned at George before getting up and walking to his bookcase.

He pulled out a copy of The Reluctant Wolf by Lisa Oliver. He brought back the hardback book he'd found and fawned over because he loved this author's gay romance books. "This book is the first one this author wrote. I have the original, but this is the limited edition hardback. I fell in love many times in the pages of her books. I always wanted a fated mate."

George came closer but kept his hands away from Scott's pride and joy, and kissed him firmly. "Seems you got what you wanted."

Scott tasted the spices from the sauce as he held George's gaze, his heart running wild in his chest. "It seems I truly did." And Scott couldn't find a thing wrong with that, de-spite the mess surrounding him.

Sometimes, miracles do happen.

You had to spoil it.

No, you just did by not giving me the last word!

Chapter Fourteen

George

"Fucking entitled bastard," George muttered under his breath as his fare stumbled out of the cab, leaving his pristine new car full of the fumes of the very liquid lunch the man had clearly enjoyed. Door slammers deserved their own version of hell, in George's opinion—one where they got subjected to automatic slamming doors, landing on their heads every five minutes.

Inhaling sharply and letting the breath out slowly, George checked the time on his dashboard clock. It was only three in the afternoon. *Another hour to go until I pick up Scott.* George knew a lot of his foul mood was because of his mating. *Whoever made up the spiel about mating being a perfect meld of two completely different people hadn't factored an OCD demon into the mix.*

Putting his car into gear, George moved into traffic, just mindlessly following the car ahead of him. He hadn't flicked his sign to indicate he was available for a fare. Knowing his luck, he'd end up being snagged by some idiot with a dozen bags who wanted to go to the airport, or even the next town over, which had happened the day before. George wasn't sure what upset him more—the fact he only got a five-dollar tip, or that Scott hadn't even noticed he was almost an hour late turning up at his work to collect him.

It's not all bad. George wasn't sure who he was trying to convince. His bear was firmly on Team Scott and couldn't work out why they didn't just camp in the demon's office. George knew he couldn't handle doing that all day, and besides, Scott never mentioned the possibility, anyway.

Scott was up bright and early every morning, his hair perfect, his suit sharp, and ready to leave for the office by eight.

George was more of a "wake up when I feel like it" and pre-ferred to have three coffees before he made his way out of the house in the morning. That wasn't possible anymore because... of Scott.

To help his bear feel better about their separation, George offered to take Scott to work every morning and pick him up in the evening instead of Scott using Dakata's driver. It was a compromise.

It wouldn't be so bad if it wasn't for Scott's need to con-trol every aspect of normal dust everyday living incurred. George found himself heading in the direction of his house and decided it would be a good idea to check on his things. There was no way he could have more than three changes of clothing at Scott's place... and no, George would nev-er consider Scott's penthouse his home, even though his mate lived there.

He shook his head, remembering a random comment he'd made three nights before about how it would be nice if he could have a few of his things at Scott's place. His feet were chilly on Scott's wooden floor, although it was more of a comfort thing than anything else. It's not that he needed the slippers—it was the principle the slippers represent-ed.

George wished he'd kept his mouth shut. Scott started hyperventilating, immediately running to his closet, trying to work out how he could create more storage to account for George's items. At the end of an exhausting hour watching Scott basically fall to pieces, organizing and reorganizing more suits than any man needed to have, George physically pulled him away from the closet, got him on the bed and kissed him senseless. After all that, George ended up with three empty clothes hangers for his clothes.

"It's not like you need any more clothes," Scott had said brightly, his eyes still anxious. "I can zap you anything else you need."

It wasn't that George wasn't welcome at Scott's apartment—he was. Anytime he mentioned perhaps they could stay at his place for a day or two, Scott just shook his head. In his head, George was safer in the penthouse, although George noted—privately, of course—that Scott never seemed to care where he went every day. *To the point of not noticing if I'm late.*

Parking outside of his house, George felt a pang as he took in the tidy exterior and gardens. He paid one of the local teenagers to take care of his lawns and pull out the odd weed, so from the outside it always looked maintained, even if he was away a week or more.

Making his way up the path, George opened the front door, inhaling deeply as he walked inside, closing the door behind him.

Home. The feeling hit him like a punch to the chest. George made his way over to his huge, plush couch, slumping on the cushions, deliberately throwing a couple of the pillows onto the floor. They looked like a bright invitation to go rolling on his rug, although he knew Scott wouldn't see things that way.

There was still a hint of Scott's scent in the air, and George groaned as he rolled around so he was lying on the couch, staring at his ceiling.

Scott can't help the way he is. You saw the home he grew up in.

Actually, George hadn't seen much of Scott's parents' home at all—he'd been too busy chasing demons down the stairs. Except somehow, in Scott's mind, he equated his pristine surroundings as his way of having control over his space, of being seen as successful in a chaotic world. George wished his sweet mate could see how he looked in George's eyes—amazing, successful and so damn sexy when he let go of his anxiety for five minutes. When the demon melted in his arms...

No good thinking about that right now. George glanced at the clock. He still had half an hour to go before he was due to pick Scott up.

I could have a shower.

George closed his eyes and groaned again. The shower was becoming another main point of contention between them. Scott's shower had glass walls, bright chrome fixtures, and glorious water pressure. In the time George had been staying with his mate, he couldn't recall one time when he'd had a shower without Scott lurking outside of it, waiting with a spray cleaning bottle and cloth in hand.

"You can come in with me if you like." George remembered the first time he'd mentioned it. He was always up for sexy times, and the idea of Scott's wet body pressed up against his was enough to get his cock to perk up. But Scott's look of absolute horror was the fastest track to droops-ville he'd ever experienced, at least for George's poor cock.

"The cleaning products will upset your bear's nose," Scott had explained, totally getting the wrong idea, as if George's cock hadn't been waving at him thirty seconds before. "I can wait until you're finished."

And so yeah, any chance George had of just relaxing the stiffness from his muscles, stemming from being in the taxi all day, got lost due to Scott's horror at water leaving marks on his bright clean surfaces.

Heaving himself off his couch, George went through into his bedroom, smiling ruefully at the half a dozen pillows and cushions still sprinkled across his bed, and into the bathroom.

"Hello, watermarks, my old friend," he murmured, reaching into his shower and turning on the water. His shower-head wasn't as powerful as the one at Scott's place, but it did the job. Shucking off his clothes, smirking at his second mini rebellion for the afternoon, he dropped them on the floor.

George stepped into the spray, turning so that the water pelted on his back. "Ah, yes, this is what I needed." George sighed as he felt his back muscles relax. He hadn't realized just how tense he'd become living with Scott.

It wasn't just the shower or Scott's uncomfortable couch. It was all the little things, like having to wash and dry his coffee cup every time he used one or making sure his clothes were put in his bag, or the washing hamper the absolute second he took them off. If George didn't do it, then Scott was there, zipping around behind him and cleaning up after him as if he was an errant toddler. George didn't like the way that made him feel, but he really wasn't sure what he could do about it.

I should go and spend some time in the forest tomorrow, let my bear have a run, George decided as he wet his hair and reached for his shampoo. *Get some mud between my claws, a few twigs in my fur, and maybe roll around a bit in the grass just because I can.*

Shifting was another thing George didn't like to suggest to his mate he needed to do. Scott wouldn't say no. He never did. *No, the damn man would probably follow me with one of those mini vacs and a brush, trying to keep my fur clean.* Chuckling, because George didn't think Scott was that bad, or at least he hoped not, he washed his hair out and shut off the water.

"My goodness," he said in a false high tone as he stepped out onto the tiles. "There's water drips on the floor!" He laughed again at his own nonsense, swiping at his discarded shirt with his foot and smushing the shirt over the drips. "And now it's clean again."

Dry and primped as much as George would ever be, he wandered back into his bedroom and pulled out a fresh shirt and pants. *I wonder if Scott will even notice I changed my shirt?* He checked his reflection in the mirror. His reflection was shaking his head. Unfortunately, for all Scott's attention to detail when it came to his work and his fastidiousness about keeping the house clean, when it came to his mate, it was as if Scott barely noticed him at all.

"It's still early days yet." George saluted his reflection and went through the house again, picking up his keys and heading out the door. Locking up behind himself, George had a sinking feeling that it wouldn't matter how long he and Scott were together, Scott was always going to prefer his pristine living space and his work duties to spending time with his scruffy mate.

Chapter Fifteen

Scott

Whatever was going on with George—Scott felt there was something—a block prevented him from finding out what it was. His mate had been an hour late the day before and Scott hadn't wanted to make a fuss, mating was about finding balance. Wasn't it?

Was he balanced? Not in the damn slightest. Something his demon kept pointing out every time Scott's anxiousness took charge.

You'll drive him away with your pernickety behavior. Our poor honey bear can't relax for a moment without you fussing every time he does something.

I am not fussing!

You followed him into the bathroom, cleaner in hand, and when he offered for us to get in with him, you gave him some baloney about the spray upsetting his bear's nose.

Well, it would. Those chemicals could be harsh. There was no way he wanted to inflict that on his blissful one.

He was inviting us to shower with him, not for you to spray that cleaner on the glass to get rid of water spots. How can we be connected when you don't notice when our honey bear has something else in mind? He doesn't want you cleaning every five minutes. Why won't you listen to me?

Was I really that bad?

His demon rolled his eyes at him and started to recite everything he'd done since George had moved in with them—sort of.

It took five minutes and Scott's stomach was rocking and rolling like he was cast out to sea on a tiny bit of wood, trying to keep his balance. He *was* fussing, oh, to the demon gods.

Shoulders sagging, he trudged into Christa's office—or Luka's, or was it Merihem's again, since Christa had disappeared without a word—a file that contained the new contracts he'd typed up ready for a signature from Merihem. The other demon had come in because of Christa's lack of appearance, not that anyone seemed too concerned, so Scott kept his thoughts and questions to himself. He had enough on his plate if he was as bad as his demon side believed.

Was that why George had been late the day before? Was he needing more time away from Scott and his fussy nature?

"Why do you look so glum?" Merihem was alone, Luka having left to go and visit a band across town an hour ago. "You found your blissful one, you should be on cloud nine."

He sounded so smug and looked so happy, Scott scowled at his boss. "I am," he snapped, totally out of character.

Merihem's gaze narrowed on him, and he blushed, realizing how he sounded. "Sorry. I have a lot on my mind."

"So it would seem." Merihem pointed to the seat in front of the large desk he was sitting behind. "Sit."

Scott wanted to object, knowing that George would arrive soon, if he wasn't late again. He'd happily stand outside in the rain and wait so as not to inconvenience his mate.

Except, this was his boss, and Scott was nothing if not a professional—if he discounted the one moment of snappiness.

When he had taken the seat, Merihem gave him a careful look. "You aren't happy." It wasn't a question, more an observation, one Scott didn't feel the need to answer. "Has this got anything to do with your family?"

Scott jerked upright.

What had Merihem heard?

Being Controller for the demon and human realm, he suspected there was little Merihem didn't know. "What have you heard?" he asked, sounding choked.

Had his family done as they said they would and gone to the king?

Not that the king could do anything to change his status. Could he? The thought dug right in, and Scott's panic at not being everything he should be was there, waiting to emerge. Did Merihem have instructions on how to deal with the issue? Was that why he'd come to the office today?

Stop being foolish. Merihem works here.

Did the rational comment help? Did it hell! How could it, when Scott was terrified of losing what he held most precious over everything—George?

"Your family is well known in the demon realm for their... views on certain things."

That was the polite way of saying they were snobbish assholes. Scott didn't need Merihem to tell him, but had they been to see the king? "Have they been to see the king?"

Merihem, who up to this point had looked amused, now gave him a look that was indeterminate. "Not that I am aware. Why would they want to speak to the king?"

Scott debated for a few seconds, staring at Merihem. The other demon wasn't someone he'd ever have considered confiding in. Except, with Dakata in the forest, what choice did he have? It wasn't like he had any friends, and George wasn't an option. "My parents aren't happy that I have a blissful one who is a bear."

"So, it's none of their damn business. Fate chose George for you as a perfect match."

The second the words left Merihem's mouth, and they sank in, Scott was up and pacing. "You see, that's it, right there. How can we be perfect for each other when I can't seem to make my blissful one happy with my..." he blushed to his roots, but kept going and avoided looking at Merihem using his demon's word, "fussing."

Merihem didn't laugh, and that helped when he came forward, resting his elbows on the desk. "Fussing? You might need to explain that a bit more."

Scott continued to pace. "My childhood gave me a few issues with control." *A few!*

Will you leave me to have my personal breakdown over here alone? No one needs comments from the peanut gallery!

"You mean your anal tendencies with having everything orderly?"

"Anal?" he fired back indignantly, "I'm not anal."

You are.

Merihem rose and walked to the office door. "Come with me."

Scott frowned but followed, unsure why they needed to leave the office. He stopped at the door of Scott's office. He pointed inside. "Tell me what you see?"

Back was the frown, and he was starting to wonder why he'd picked Merihem to talk to. He glanced inside and saw nothing out of place. Just how he liked it. "What am I looking for?"

Merihem walked in, went to his desk, and moved a stack of orderly papers. Scott was right behind him, tutting and shifting them back.

"You're like Peni."

Scott stopped what he was doing to return his attention to Merihem. "What do you mean?" Peni was a pygmy goat, not a demon.

"Peni likes things orderly. Neat. His childhood was full of chaos, and it shaped him. In the beginning, he struggled with how messy I was, especially when I didn't understand his need to clean up after me. That he couldn't shift his attention—unless I gave him something else to occupy him—from the mess. It stresses him."

As Merihem spoke, Scott found he could relate to Peni's feelings.

"Does George do anything to distract you? Help you take your mind off the *perceived messiness*?"

Back to blushing, he found it hard to meet Merihem's amused gaze, when he clearly used the same technique on Peni when Scott nodded. Then it struck what he'd said, 'perceived messiness.' Did George think him fussy or anal?

You're both.

Thanks!

"I think you should talk with my blissful one. He's got a lot in common with your view on things. He might be able to help… give you some pointers."

Scott eyed Merihem intrigued by the idea. Despite being uncomfortable discussing such things with others, he was desperate. Point in case he was talking to Merihem, who, up until meeting Peni, most definitely hadn't worried about wearing clothes or who he fucked and where. Scott had heard all the rumors the same as everyone else about Merihem.

He'd changed. Did that mean Scott could change? Be whatever it was that would make George remove the wall between them?

He nodded and checked his watch. "I've got half an hour before George arrives, would now be a good time?"

Merihem stood in silence for a few seconds, then Peni appeared looking flushed and holding a cleaning cloth. "You could have given me another minute to put my cloth in the washer." He nodded shyly at Scott, tucking the cloth into the back pocket of his jeans. "Merihem said you'd like to have a chat."

"If you have a few minutes and wouldn't mind."

"Of course, Merihem can finish off what I was doing when we go home."

Merihem chuckled and kissed the tip of Peni's nose. That he had to bend nearly in half didn't seem to faze him, or that he had an audience for his show of affection. "Anything for you, my love."

Scott glanced at Merihem and arched a brow when Merihem showed no sign of leaving.

"Alright," he groused, shaking his head, heading back out of the office and shutting the door.

Peni looked about the office and grinned widely. "You are not like Merihem at all."

Scott once more examined his space and huffed. "No, but it seems that being like this for my blissful one isn't good, if I listen to my demon."

"Oh..." Peni stared at him. "Is he like Merihem, a little messy and disorganized? Or is it worse than that?"

On that, he had to think. "His place is more... disorganized, and I suppose, a little chaotic. It's clean, but nothing appears to have a right place to go." Was it disrespectful to talk about such things about his blissful one? "My home, everything has a place. When something is used, I expect those things to get cleaned and put back into an orderly fashion."

Peni took a seat and gave him a thoughtful look. "Was your home life as disruptive as mine?"

"I'm not sure what you mean by that?" Scott took the seat next to Peni. "My family… is that what you mean?" At the nod, he continued on. "They remain disappointed in me," he confessed for the first time.

"How so? I look at you and I see someone who seems to know what he wants, is successful, and has a life he has chosen."

"I am. I've worked hard to make them see me on the same level as them."

Peni tilted his head to the side. "Level? I'm not sure what you mean?"

"I'm a pale blue demon, who looks nothing like my family. My siblings. I've been a constant source of ridicule for my family since I was born. I… I overcompensate." Even as he said it, Scott got the magnitude of those words. He overcompensated in all areas of his life, work… home… *shit!*

He was overcompensating with George too. Trying to prove he was worthy, despite what George said. His bear had not once shown he wasn't worthy. He'd gone toe to toe with his parents when they were awful towards him. Not George, *but him*.

Now we're getting somewhere.

As that sank in, he voiced his deepest fear. "I'm trying to overcompensate with my blissful one..."

Peni rubbed a hand on the sleeve of his suit jacket. "Because of your family, and you're worried he'll reject you."

Scott's breath whistled through his teeth as he nodded his agreement. His whole life was about rejection. If he wasn't perfect for George, in Scott's mind, it stood to reason he would reject him, just like his family.

"I understand that. I need everything to be clean and in its right place because my dad had sex everywhere in the house. Dirtied everything. He wanted me to be like him and rut right alongside him, uncaring how I felt about it. Merihem understands my quirks, and I'm learning when it's okay to not obsess." He glanced at the closed door, grinning, before his expression went back to serious. "Have you talked to George? Explained how hard it is for you?"

He shook his head. "I haven't, because I feel this barrier between us," Scott confessed. "So, I try harder to be perfect for him."

Making matters worse.

Peni gave him a sympathetic smile. "It's hard sometimes explaining how things are. But George seems like a nice bear, so maybe you should have a talk to him, too... about this."

With that in mind, Scott tidied his desk twenty minutes later and headed down to meet George with a promise that if he needed to talk again Peni would listen to him.

The new cab pulled up to the curb, and Scott smiled brightly at George, who wore a more half smile, not appearing as happy as Scott to see him.

There was the wall, and Scott's heart jammed against his ribs and remained there. He slipped into the seat next to George. His smile dimmed, and he frowned when he noted the shirt George wore was not the one he'd had on that morning. Scott didn't miss that his bear had recently had a shower and had not used the body wash in Scott's home.

His buoyed mood over the conversation plummeted. "I'm doing this all wrong," he wailed and promptly started to sob, his emotions all over the place with his insecurities.

Chapter Sixteen

George

"The situation is getting worse," George said glumly, sitting shirtless in the forest with twigs in his hair. Dougal, sitting across from him, handed him a mug filled with cider. George had his run in his bear form, which wasn't as helpful as he'd hoped, as his bear kept wanting to head back to town to camp outside Scott's door.

"This mating business is supposed to be all love and sexy times, right? Two people connected on a soul deep level, never having to explain themselves because their other half gets them completely."

"I think it takes a bit more work than that." Dougal chuckled. "If you think about it, from a totally academic perspective..."

"Since when were you an academic?" George managed a smile for his friend.

"I have my skills. But humor me here. You have a situation where two complete strangers suddenly realize, through scent, blood, or magic, that they are meant to be together forever. A Fates' pairing that will stop a paranormal from being lonely for the rest of their long existence."

"I'm not so sure a blissful one means the same thing to demons," George became compelled to point out. "Scott's mind is so busy with his work and keeping things organized, he doesn't even miss me through the day. Whereas my bear spent the past hour trying to get me to go back to town, just so he could be with his demon. It's a physical strain on me every day being apart from him."

"So be with him." Dougal shrugged. "Being mated is all about compromise. Going back to what I was saying from an academic standpoint, the closeness the Fates ensure all shifters feel for their other halves is a means of fostering that connection—ensuring you learn to live with your mate in a way that makes you both happy."

"Yes, well, when I picked Scott up from work last night, he burst into tears within seconds of getting into the cab. You tell me. Is that the sign of a happy demon?"

Dougal stretched out his legs and took a swig from his mug. "Did you ask him why he was so upset?"

"Of course I did. What type of bear do you take me for?" George shook his head. "My other half was ready to fur out and storm into that fancy office space of his and tear everyone to shreds for upsetting my mate. But Scott wouldn't let me. He was sobbing about how he was doing everything wrong, and I didn't know if he was talking about contracts, spreadsheets, or the way he made the bed that morning. It's not like I can get any sense out of him when he gets upset that way. He had a complete meltdown, and that's not the first time it's happened."

"Sounds to me like a stressed-out demon who's feeling insecure about his mating bond."

George stared at his friend in shock. "You're kidding me, right? You think this is all my fault?"

"No." Dougal shook off George's concern with a deep chuckle. "I think from what you've said about Scott before, he's feeling stressed because he doesn't think he's good enough for you."

Snorting, George said, "You have seen him, haven't you? Gorgeous, immaculate, successful, well-off, highly respected demon—the one who had the unfortunate luck to be mated to a scruffy bear. That Scott?"

"There's more to you than the twigs in your hair," Dougal pointed out. "But it seems to me that for a demon who strives for perfection in absolutely everything he does, he is going to reach breaking point at some time. It's not possible for anyone to achieve the high standards he sets himself every freaking time. It'd be exhausting. But tell me, what happened when you got him home? Did he calm down? Talk to you about why he was upset?"

"Oh, I wish." George was still trying to come to terms with what he'd seen, and he'd been there. "He stalked into his penthouse, and remember how I told you he has doors on his bookcase so that things look streamlined and clean? Well, he pulls on those doors so hard one of them comes off its hinges. Next thing I know, there are cushions and books and throw rugs flying everywhere, all over the floor. Scott is still crying, mind you, sobbing about how he can do this, and he will do this, and…"

George shook his head. "There was a huge mess, and I could see just by looking at him it was really stressing Scott out. Before I could say anything or help him pick anything up, he stripped off his clothes with a click of his fancy fingers, and then I was swept up like a bride in a fantasy story, rushed off to the bedroom where I'm sure Scott was trying to get under my skin, he was that desperate to be close to me.

"I'm not saying that wasn't wonderful, because times like that with Scott always are, but he was back, scrubbing his floors and tidying everything away the moment he thought I was asleep. That really gutted me, and this morning, he was just like he always is, dressed before me, eager to get to work—eager to get away from me is how I see it."

"Sounds like you two need to sit down and have a serious talk," Dougal said, and he sounded genuinely concerned. "Compromise isn't all about one person giving into the needs of their partner, which you both sound like you're doing with disastrous effects. Compromise is where the two of you work out how much you can each bend to meet together in the middle, where you'll both be happy, instead of breaking apart."

"That's what I thought it was, too. Except Scott didn't notice that I'd showered back at my place yesterday, he never said anything about me being late to pick him up the day before." George felt tears prick his eyes, and he blinked them away. "And I know what you're going to say—that it's my fault Scott feels he can't talk to me, although I can't think what I've said or done to make him feel that way."

"I didn't say it was your fault, but Scott can't help the way he is either," Dougal reminded him. "He was the way he is a long time before he met you, and fair to say, you're the same. I'm not hearing any sign of the two of you talking to each other…"

"How can I without making him feel bad about himself?" George stopped a moment, inhaling slowly and letting his breath out again before continuing in a quieter voice. "If I mention anything about how Scott doesn't need to wipe down the shower the moment I get out of it, or how I don't mind a coffee mug being rinsed and left on the counter, he gets this shuttered look on his face, as though I'm making a personal attack against him.

"He actually shuts right down, and talking to him then is just a waste of time because as I'm flapping my gums, trying to get through to him, he's thinking about how long he has to pretend he's listening to me before he can go back to cleaning again. You say he's exhausted. I'm exhausted, too. I can't live up to his ideal of household perfection. It's getting so I don't even dare fart in bed in case he bounds out of my arms and runs off to find an air freshener."

"A holiday could be a good idea for you both," Dougal suggested, his lips pursing in thought.

"Separately, you mean? I doubt there's a hotel, motel, or cabin in existence that would meet Scott's idea of what a clean living space actually means."

George leaned forward, resting his elbows on his knees. "I was thinking the other day we could go on one of those fancy cruises—you know, the ones where the rooms are kept clean by discreet staff, and food is all laid out, and all we'd have to do is enjoy the sun and visit far off locations. No responsibilities, no devices or phones. Just eat, drink, have some laughs, and yes, talk to each other as well. But I doubt I have a crowbar big enough to separate Scott from the office. Being organized there is the key part of his existence. It would be like me cutting off one of his limbs to take him away from that."

"The thing is, you don't know that." Dougal pointed a finger at him. "You're making a lot of assumptions about him and what he's thinking, and I'll bet you a double meat burger he's doing the same thing about you. That has to be the case because neither one of you is talking to the other, and yet you both think you know what your mate—blissful one—is thinking. Can't you see where that's a bit twisted?"

"Yeah, you'll be right about that, I reckon." George glanced up, noting where the sun was in relation to the horizon, and put his mug next to the log he was sitting on. "The thing is, I haven't got a clue what to do about it. I don't want to hurt my mate—that's the last thing on my mind. But I can't live like a blow-up doll with a glued-hair helmet, and sterile clothes either. I could be wrong. Perhaps Scott adores his life, and it's me he has the problem with. By the same token, he could've forgotten how to have fun entirely and needs me to help him find his joy again. I haven't got a clue."

Standing up, George reached for his shirt and tugged it over his head, smoothing it down and then picking out the odd twig he could feel in his hair. "If you can think of a way that I could talk to my mate without causing him to have a meltdown, or without hurting him, I'd be grateful for the advice. For now, I'd better get back. Scott might not notice when I'm late picking him up, but you can guarantee my bear is going to give me grief about it if I'm not on time."

"You need to get him out of his perfect office and out of his perfect house," Dougal suggested. "Take a holiday, take time to talk to each other, spend time together instead of this stupid routine you've got going on, because that's not working for either one of you."

"Sound advice, my friend, but forgive me if I think I'd have more luck winning a lottery I don't have a ticket for than getting Scott out of his office." George huffed out a long breath. "Thanks for listening. I don't know where you get all your good ideas from, seeing as I can't remember any time when you've been in a relationship yourself, but it's appreciated."

"I have—had a special someone in my life once who thought their position was more important than a solid relationship with someone who adored them." Dougal shrugged. "As you see," he spread his arms, indicating the clearing, "I'm still alone. I don't want to see that happen to you and your demon. This forest already has a resident loner, and that's me. You need to find a way to talk to your mate. It's as simple and as difficult as that."

"Finding the time would be a good start," George agreed, saluting his friend as he walked off.

He was more than happy to agree with Dougal that he'd been making assumptions about Scott and that he could be wrong about him.

In George's eyes, actions always spoke louder than words, and every time Scott reached for a cleaning cloth, instead of just enjoying the closeness with his blissful one, George felt shut out of Scott's life more and more.

This can't go on, he thought as he made his way back to his cab.

Chapter Seventeen

Scott

He blew his nose into the tissue that Peni had given him when he'd arrived and been unable to hold back the tears when Peni opened the door to Dakata's old home. Now Merihem's and Peni's. He had managed to keep it together until lunchtime, then the sandwich George had made for him set him off. So, he had rung Peni and was now sitting at their kitchen table, crying.

Merihem had escaped after taking one look at his blood-shot, puffy eyes and hadn't come back. "I'm so sorry, but I needed someone to talk to, and you did offer," he sobbed, feeling the need to repeat that even after Peni said it was fine. Doing his best to hold in the next bout of tears, he wiped at his drippy nose. "It's just I don't know what to do."

Peni patted his hand. "It's okay. Would you like a cup of coffee? Tea?"

"Tea would be nice." Scott hoped that while Peni made it, he would be able to pull himself together. All his grand plans the evening before had gone up in hell's fire when the tears had started in the cab. George had looked so lost. Confused almost, but how, Scott didn't understand. Then Scott had gotten home and—well, for want of a better word—went crazy.

Inside the apartment, he needed to show George that he could be everything he wanted and needed. He didn't give himself time to think about his actions. He stomped into his orderly living space and started grabbing things and throwing them around. His books, his pillows, and the blankets he'd gotten for George.

"Scott, honey, what are you doing?" George questioned from the doorway looking at Scott like he'd not seen him before in his life.

"Can't you see," he sobbed. "I'm making it better. Showing you, I can be the way you want. Need." He'd gotten into his stride, blocking his demon, who was making strange noises in his mind.

"Honey, you don't need to do this." George came into the room, his worried gaze tracking Scott, who was knee deep in mess.

"I do," he declared, although he couldn't look at what he'd done. Instead, he clicked his fingers, and naked, he stalked to George, aroused, and lifted him clear off the floor. Scooping him into his arms, his demon was back on board with what was going to happen next. He kissed George with all the feelings he had, praying it was enough to make George understand he was everything Scott wanted.

"Want to tell me what happened?" Peni asked, jarring him from his thoughts and stopping his thoughts from traveling to what happened next.

"I lost it." He went with that because it was probably the best place to start.

Peni twisted to look at him from the kitchen counter where he was making the tea. "Lost what?"

"My damn mind." He sniffed and dabbed at his wet eyes. "I was going to talk to George, you know, like we discussed, then when I got in the cab to go home." He sniffed indignantly. "He'd changed his shirt and had a shower," Scott stated, once more back to feeling miserable.

"I'm sorry, I'm not seeing why this is a problem?" Peni came over with the mug, and a small jug of milk, placing both in front of Scott, giving him an apologetic look, before he pushed the small bowl of sugar towards the black tea.

Scott released a heavy sigh and tried to make himself understood because his demon was being no help. He had shut himself off from Scott in such a way he actually couldn't feel his presence. Scary and totally not what Scott needed, so he'd closed himself off, too, because one hurt to deal with at a time was enough. "George had gone back to his home before he came to collect me from work. He had showered and changed his shirt before he came to meet me. It could only be because he doesn't like me following him into the shower to clean up after him. Just like my demon said. I'm driving him away." He sniffed, willing the ache in his eyes away. "Anyway, I got a little upset."

Peni took a seat and added milk to his own tea. "Because he had a shower in his own place?"

Scott nodded. "I tried to be messy. I did. I pulled stuff out and messed up the place, wanting him to see I could be what he needed."

"Ohh…"

A hiccup sob came out as he sagged in the seat at how Peni looked and sounded, suspecting he was only just realizing Scott had, in fact, jumped off the deep end of crazy. "I couldn't find the words when George didn't seem to know how to react. That just made it worse." Scott blushed, recalling that it wasn't all bad, because seriously, what happened in the bedroom was… yes, it wasn't all bad. Except when he had woken after the sex, his mind had gone all squirrely on him about how much of a mess he'd made, then he got up to fix it, and he explained to Peni, "When I did that, the wall was back between me and George."

There were a few seconds of silence as Peni observed him from over the lip of his mug. "It's hard trying to be perfect all the time, I bet."

"It is," he admitted. "I just don't know how to switch it off."

Peni tapped at the mug he held. "Maybe switching it off isn't the key. What about dialing it down? You know, like turning the dial down on the radio when a song grates on your ears."

Scott sipped at the hot black tea. He scowled as the tea burned the back of his throat when he swallowed, making him realize he'd not used the milk. He placed the mug down and sighed. "How do I do that?"

"I'm not sure how 'cause really, to start with, you have to talk about how you're feeling. The fears you got tucked inside. They might be what's turning your dial up." He blushed and glanced at the doorway, and Scott sensed Merihem was just outside it listening to them.

He was past caring about being embarrassed. The meltdown he had at work with Luka, who had messed up his desk looking for a file, something he never thought himself capable of, was what had driven him to leave work and seek Peni.

Peni took another sip of his tea and hummed. "Sometimes we need others to tell us when we are escalating. Then we can stop, take a moment, and figure out what set us off. Or do something different to help distract us."

He let what Peni said sink in, and Scott, now a little calmer, could see that there was truth in what Peni was saying. His dial had gotten pushed up to its limit a long time ago, and he needed ways to bring it down. Positive ways that didn't make him feel like a failure. George was good at helping, but then he messed that up, overreacting when his brain re-engaged. "I need to talk to George and not overreact. That's the first step."

Peni gave him an encouraging smile. "I think that's a great first step."

His chat with Peni boosted him, so when he returned to work, Scott was able to concentrate. He managed to get everything done for Luka, who kept giving him odd looks, which Scott ignored. It wasn't every day he lost his cool. In some way, it felt a little cathartic almost, that he had opened a valve inside to let out some of the pressure.

So, as he tidied up his things, Scott was feeling more positive than earlier in the day. He checked everything was off before he picked up his laptop bag to sling it over his shoulder. In the elevator, he didn't speak to the couple of men he recognized, aware his eyes were still a little puffy and bloodshot.

Scott couldn't lie to George, but he hoped the chilled cucumber slices he had used in the restroom would deter questions George might have. He nodded at the security guards as he exited the building, checking his watch as he glanced at the place George used to park and saw it was empty.

He was a minute or two early, so Scott walked to the bench in the tiny green area—it couldn't be classed as a garden as it was a patch of artificial grass with no flowers—just off to the side that gave him a good view of the street. Scott plucked out his phone as he sat and scrolled a little through emails and used the time to file them in the appropriate files he had for storing correspondence when finished.

Time ticked on and Scott watched the minutes pass by as he considered if George had gone home again. He sighed at the thought. The sky started to darken, and Scott shivered, a sense of foreboding growing in the pit of his stomach.

Can you sense George?

Answer me!

George is really late, and I'm worried about him.

Crickets.

Please. I need to know if he's okay. Maybe he just got caught up, and I'm worried about nothing.

An hour and a half later, Scott had a throbbing headache and was losing patience with his demon's lack of response. *If something happens to our blissful one, then I'm going to hold you responsible,* he snarled loudly, making his own ears ring.

He felt his demon surge forward and, expecting him to grump for shouting, Scott became shocked and stood frozen when his demon started crying. *I'm so sorry.*

What... w-what w-wrong!

I can't feel him.

Ears ringing with how fast his heart was racing, Scott shook from the terror coming from his demon. *At all?*

No.

I feel nothing through our bond, his demon cried pitifully.

Holy fuck.

Holy fuck.

Holy fuck.

Georgeeeeee!

Chapter Eighteen

George

"What the ever-loving fuck?" George slapped at his neck, the hand from his passenger in the back touching him, giving him an ick feeling. George thought he felt the prick of a fingernail as well, *asshole.* "No distracting the driver."

George was already distracted enough. Scenes from the night before scrolled through his mind on an endless loop. George was seeking clues, moments, opportunities he might have missed to make things better for his unhappy mate. So maybe he wasn't being conversationalist of the year for his paying customers, but they paid him to drive, not listen to their life story.

"Just being friendly. You seem like a fun guy to get to know."

"I've got my driver's license. You don't need to know anything else."

"Oh, I don't know. With those brawny arms and that sexy beard, I reckon there's a lot of things we could learn about each other."

Yeah, the guy was a complete creep. Not that George was paying any attention to him. It was just an assumption he'd made from the moment the guy had gotten into the car—one of those gut feelings that George got at times, where he couldn't be assed to talk to his passengers. His only job was to get them to where they needed to go. If he only transported passengers he could actually stand to have a conversation with, he'd spend his day driving around alone.

Checking the time on his dashboard, George carefully increased the speed just a little. He should make it. The creep wanted to go to an address George knew was out by the airport, so half an hour with afternoon traffic, and another thirty minutes back into town. He should be pulling into the parking lot with five minutes to spare.

"Take this turnoff, coming up on the left." The passenger was leaning in the gap between the seats, and George scowled at him in the rear vision mirror.

"The turnoff for the address you wanted is another two miles down the road."

"This way's a shortcut. You can drop me off at the back of the property because this road goes around that way."

Another tight ass. George flicked on his indicator. If he had a dollar for every time someone tried to convince him to take a shortcut—well, he had enough money as it was, it would buy a nice holiday for him and Scott.

The more he thought about it, the more George wanted to take his mate on holiday. He wanted Scott to be okay. It was so hard making out that everything was all hunky dory, as they got ready for work that morning. *Did he even like the sandwich I made him? Did he take the time off needed to eat it?* He hoped Scott would see that for what it was—a way of George trying to show he was supportive of his mate in all things.

I'll kiss him when I pick him up this afternoon, he decided. To hell with appearances and worrying if that sort of behavior would be considered respectful to the people

Scott worked with. His mate needed to know he was cared about, even if Scott did get a bit crazy every now and then. It wasn't like George was perfect.

The road they were traveling down definitely wasn't on any map George had seen before. It was barely a road at all. He cursed as the bottom of his new cab scraped on the gravel after his wheel hit one of the many potholes and he slowed down. The road was more pothole than anything else. "Are you sure you want to go down this way?" he asked, glancing at the man in his mirror.

The man's smirk sent a shiver down George's spine. "It might not have been this turnoff, after all. But it's okay. There's a small space where you can turn around just up ahead. Sorry, about that."

Idiot. Fucking wasting my time. George glanced at the clock again. He could still make it, but he'd have to push it heading back to town.

The turnaround appeared out of nowhere, causing George to brake and lurch forward. *Damn it. This is going to be tight.* He spun the wheel hard to the left, barely applying any pressure on the accelerator at all. He heard the brush of bushes against his paintwork and cursed again under his breath. His new car was not what one could consider an off-road vehicle.

But no, the turn was too tight. Backing up just a smidge, George turned his wheel hard again, shaking his head as a sudden attack of wooziness made him lose focus for a moment.

Bear! Struggling with the wheel and the tight turn, George screamed out at his animal side… but there was nothing there.

"Having a bit of trouble… *bear*?"

"You?" Slamming on the brakes, George turned in his seat. "You did something to me when you fondled my neck. Get out of my fucking car."

Fuck, he could barely stay upright, clinging to the steering wheel one-handed as the passenger, still smirking, opened his door and got out. "I think you might need some help there, bear." The man wrenched open George's door before he'd even had a chance to turn around, and then those same hands were on George's arm, pulling him out of the vehicle.

He was powerless to stop the asshole, but George wasn't going to go down quietly. He lashed out with his fists and feet, kicking and punching the man anytime he got close. All he could think was that Scott would be waiting for him, and he was not going to let his mate down.

There was a crunch of bone as George got in at least one good hit, but the man was a fucking maniac and kept coming back. Whatever George had been injected with was taking him over, making his limbs heavier, his coordination was shot to hell, and he was getting spots in front of his eyes. He pushed out his energy with everything he had. He couldn't let Scott down. But the man kept coming, and then George felt another prick in his neck and went down like a fallen tree.

All he could hear as he passed out was the man's laughter.

Chapter Nineteen

Scott

Scott had never known terror like it, it took him seconds to get a breath into his chest. To make it expand and stop the obscene tightness from taking his wobbling legs from under him.

Think, goddamn it, think. Was this related to George's past? A past he'd shared but not fully because Scott remained clueless as to George's real identity. Anger came, but at himself for not pushing harder to know. George was his blissful one, this was not some trivial thing.

Is this the time to start the blaming game?

You don't even start with me. I don't have the time to have this conversation. We need to find George.

But where?

Could he have been involved in another traffic incident where someone had drugged George? He shuddered as he pulled out his phone and searched for hospitals in the area. The paramedic he'd hunted down, had he lied to Scott? Was this connected to that incident?

"Hello, St Bart's. How can I help you?"

"Yes, I'm looking to speak to my bliss—mate George May-bank?"

"Which ward is he in?" the bored-sounding woman asked sending a wave of anxiety through Scott.

"The emergency department." He would still be there if there had been an accident.

"Putting you through."

Another female voice, this one sounding more annoyed than bored, came on the phone. "How can I help you?"

"George Maybank, has he been brought in?" he asked, doing his best to sound professional and not like he was about to fall apart.

There was a sound of tapping. "When was he brought in? I have no patient in the department with that name."

Rude was not something Scott had ever been in his life, yet he ended the call and rang the next hospital.

By the seventh one, he was openly struggling to hold it together. His demon side wanted to tear the city apart, but Scott needed to be sure that they weren't missing the obvious after George's recent experience.

When he ended his final call, the sky had darkened further, and he knew without a doubt George was not in any hospital, human or shifter. He called for Miller, his last hope was that maybe George had gone to the woods to see his friend Dougal and had lost track of time. As Dougal had no phone and Scott wasn't exactly sure whereabouts he lived, he needed the car to take him to the forest.

When it drew up to a halt in front of where he was pacing, Scott's demon side started to fuss. *Let's translocate.*

We don't know where we need to go to. So, it would be like pissing in the wind trying to hit a pinhead we dropped.

I don't want to go in the car!

Listen, we don't know where Dougal lives. So, we are getting in the damn car.

Scott yanked open the door and witnessed the driver's alarmed expression as he met his gaze in the rearview mirror. "What?" he snapped, too worried about George to care if he was offending anyone.

"You've left your laptop bag on the bench?" Miller pointed to it.

In all of Scott's life, he had never shown such disregard for a possession before. He didn't even debate with himself as he muttered. "It doesn't matter, take us to the forest. The place where you would normally drop Dakata."

This was a different place from where Scott usually got dropped. He only knew that because Dakata had made reference to how he had to trudge past Dougal's. A place that Scott had never seen or been near, that he was aware of.

Miller coughed and nodded, not looking Scott in the eye. "Yes, sir."

Whatever his issue was, whether it was Scott's strange behavior or that he probably looked nothing like he usually did, Scott didn't care. He just needed to find Dougal.

This was all just a misunderstanding. George just need-ed some space after Scott's meltdown. They would talk about it in the forest like Scott should have done last night, and everything would be absolutely fine.

Lying will not change things. And we need to get out of this car!

Will you stop jabbering about the fucking car? And I'm not lying, just working to instill a little bit of fucking hope, alright! he snapped angrily. *You should just con-centrate on our link to George.*

I am, his demon sniff-sobbed, *I can't feel him. Nothing, not a thread of his essence. How are we going to find him?*

Scott had no answer, and back was the awful ball of fear growing deep in his chest that something was wrong. Really wrong.

Minutes ticked by at a pace that made each second they were in the car feel like an hour. When the car bumped its way down a potholed road before stopping by a group of large trees, Scott looked out the window.

Darkness had fully descended, and though the moon sat clear in the sky, the canopy of leaves left the forest dark.

"Wait here for me." He didn't wait for a reply as he got out, and his demon emerged. His clothes fell in ribbons to the ground, once more, none of that was a concern to Scott.

Their head lifted, and they scented the air. *I can't smell him, sense him.*

His demon sounded like a wounded animal.

Then we search until we can.

His demon took off, running through the trees, scenting the air, searching for something that would take them to George or Dougal.

Their vision was good, but as the forest grew denser, they had to slow because it became impossible to see broken tree roots and rocks. *We should be smelling something, shouldn't we?*

Scott wasn't sure how long, or how far they'd gone into the forest, but he was sure of something, they were lost. This was not the place they needed to be. There was nothing to indicate Dakata had passed this way which was puzzling. The driver had brought Dakata to the forest more than a dozen times.

I told you not to get in the car.

Why?

Something didn't feel right.

Then why weren't you more specific?

His demon snarled and the sounds of a critter scurrying away followed. He swung around in the direction they had come, not answering.

I would have listened if you were clearer.

Yeah, right.

They stayed silent as they used their scent to head back to where the car was. Only when they got there, the car was gone.

Scott's demon roared, and the branches of the surrounding trees shook violently. *Motherfucker.*

Their combined distress engulfed them, and the demon headed in the opposite direction from which they'd come. *We're going to end up going in circles.*

No, my instincts say we need to check everywhere before we leave this forest.

The force with which his demon spoke left Scott speechless.

Unsure how long they trampled through the dense trees, they came to a halt and their heart skipped a couple of beats.

Can you smell that?

George!

It was faint, but it was there. His demon closed his eyes and inhaled deeply. *I can't scent blood or death.*

Never had those words meant so much, Scott worked to control the urge to sob. *See, I was right, he's just lost track of time having fun in his bear form.*

He sensed his demon wanted to argue, but for the first time, he refrained.

Come on, we need to find him.

They took off slower than Scott would have liked, but the scent veered off and was mixed with another less familiar scent that Scott knew was Dougal's.

"What's got you clambering around these woods in the dark?" asked Dougal. Scott couldn't actually pinpoint where the voice came from until Dougal stepped out from behind a huge tree. His clothes blended with the foliage, so only the whites of his eyes were obvious.

"George, where is he?" his demon demanded impatiently.

The white disappeared, and Scott fought his demon to take control. *Where did he go?*

How the fuck do I know, his demon fired back.

Then the white was back. "George left hours ago. I can't sense him in the forest. He's not here."

They deflated, their knees buckled, and they crashed to the ground, wailing, "Georgeeeee."

"Stop that caterwauling, it won't do anyone any good."

His demon was quicker to recover, just. "Sorry. I can't sense George. It's like he's disappeared off the face of the realm."

Dougal's coat brushed the side of their arm as he hooked a hand under his. "Get up, we need to go get Dakata so he can summon Merihem. We're gonna need them all."

"For what?" they asked together as Dougal hauled them up.

"To get him out of the clutches of his family, 'cause they'll be the only ones who'd have taken him," he said, sounding way to matter-of-fact for Scott.

"You know who his family is?" The hurt left a bitter taste in Scott's mouth.

"Yes." He patted their arm. "Now, don't go getting your demon in a twist, he only told me when he'd had a little too much of my homemade brew. That could make the devil confess after two cups."

How Dougal could see where they were going, Scott didn't know and didn't care. When Dakata and Silas's house came into view, all he could think about was how Merihem had the skill to locate anyone.

Only if they're alive.

Why the hell did you have to say that? The sliver of hope that came with thoughts of help fled. All Scott could think about was how, in a few minutes, his life could be over. Because one thing was for sure, if George was dead, then Scott didn't want to live without him.

Chapter Twenty

George

George woke up with three things immediately clear. He was naked. He was bound to a metal table, and his cock was so hard it hurt. Oh, and his bear side was suppressed to the point George could feel his animal side's rage, but it was as if there was a ten-foot glass wall between them.

So technically, it was four things—five if he added in that Scott's scent was nowhere to be found. He could feel their bond, but it was muted, and as much as it pained him, George pushed it back until he could no longer feel it at all.

My dad's finally made his move, and I'm damned if I want Scott experiencing anything I'm going to go through.

It wasn't as though George hadn't expected the abduction. The incident at the hospital, even being taken to the hospital in the first place, was more than a fucking coincidence, and while George had other things on his mind with Scott, it seemed his father hadn't forgotten him at all.

Fine. If his asshole father thought he was going to cooperate with being tied down, he underestimated his only son. George had rage enough of his own, and he wasn't afraid to use it. His biceps bulged as he strained against the thick straps that were wrapped around his wrists, his upper arms, his torso, and three down each leg. He was aware he was in a sterile white environment—one Scott couldn't find fault with—but where he was didn't make any difference when the fact he was roped down like a cow for slaughter was looming hard in his mind.

Whoever built the table had bears in mind. The metal creaked as George strained, but it held firm. Furious, George's only thought was getting off that table, and if he couldn't do that, then he'd take the fucking table with him when he left.

He started rocking his body, one side and then the other. He didn't care how he fell, he just wanted his damn feet on the floor. It was giving him flashbacks—just like being in the hospital again—and George was hellbound and determined to get out of his current state just as quickly as he had from the hospital. Even if he was carrying the damn table on his back, he did not care.

"Hey, hey. Don't do that." A thin hand landed on his shoulder. "You'll knock the table over."

"Don't you dare touch me." George turned his head, glaring at a slender man in a white lab coat. The man, if lucky, was twenty if he was a day. He had a shock of blond straight hair falling over half his face and was wearing large, black-rimmed glasses that looked too big for him.

"Not touching." The man's hands both flew into the air. "Not touching you, I just didn't want you hurting your-self. You can't move this table. It's bolted to the floor."

Taking in a huge breath, George showed his teeth. "Then unbuckle me from the damn thing so I can get out of here. I've got places to be."

"Oh, I will soon." The slender man moved down the side of the table, pulling a pen out of his pocket and tapping George's cock with the end of it. "I've just got to wait for this potion to work." He shook his head. "You should've climaxed by now. It's been twenty minutes. It's very strange."

"Excuse me?" George wasn't sure if he'd heard correctly. "You're judging me because I haven't covered my belly with spunk yet?"

"Not judging. Oh, no." The man's eyes were wide behind the glasses. "I'm sure you're a very virile bear shifter." He nodded as if that added weight to his words. "It's just this potion—the lab guys have been working on it for months, it's guaranteed to make any man climax in under ten minutes."

"Even when they're unconscious?" George was angry before, but now he was literally seeing red, especially when the blond nodded as if it were a perfectly normal question.

"It's supposed to…" The man backed up, perhaps registering George's expression. "I didn't touch you, I swear. I would never touch a person without consent. That's just wrong."

"Then how…" George tried to point to his dick, but his fingers could only go so far thanks to his wrist restraints, "the hell did you cover my dick with shit? How did I get naked? Because I promise you, I was fully clothed when I got knocked out."

"I don't know anything about your clothes. That's the acquisitions department. You arrived naked. And as for the potion, they can administer it in a spray bottle now, you know, just like a hair spray."

The man was actually smiling. "There's so much concern about consent these days, so the spray bottle was a perfect idea. It's not like we want our subjects to feel uncomfortable."

Then he frowned again. "However, the potion's not working on you, which is really strange because every other subject we've tried it on, their cocks have gone off like fireworks in next to no time. I might have to give it another dose. This is very irregular."

"Don't you dare give me another zap of your shit," George growled as the man sauntered off to a large bench that ran the length of the sterile room. "I do not give you my consent!"

"I'm just spraying you, not physically touching you." The blond came back with what looked like a spray cleaning bottle. "The lab director said consent was not required unless any physical touching or invasive procedures were done, and I think that's very fair, don't you? I only have to give you two squirts."

George bellowed loud enough to raise the ceiling as his cock was assaulted with two puffs of liquid. It didn't burn, but it was as if the skin on his cock was stretching to burning point, causing his whole length to tingle. From a physical perspective, he wanted to come so badly—he could feel the sensation building in his lower belly even as his mind was screaming "*no*" with the wrongness of it all.

Just when he thought he'd totally lost control over his body, it was as if someone had slapped a cock ring around the base of his shaft and tightened it to the point of pain. The sensation was so sudden, George laughed as the need to orgasm ebbed away. "Go on, spray me again, numb-nuts. That shit's not going to work."

"My name's Ronald, not numbnuts." Ronald bent near the table, his hair within an inch of George's hand. George's fingers twitched, trying to grab it, but Ronald stayed just out of reach. "This is so very strange. Are you sure you don't want to climax?"

"Nope." George was more than happy to lie through his teeth. What he wanted was to get back to his mate and fuck him until he couldn't stand, but he didn't dare think about his precious blue demon when he was in such a precarious position. "Empty the bottle on it. It won't make any difference. You're not getting any spunk out of me, so you might as well let me go."

Ronald huffed as he straightened up. "Can't you just think some sexy thoughts and give your cock a boost for me? I need one pottle's worth, that's all. I don't know what sort of thoughts you need to… you know," he waved at his head, "think. But if you just—"

"All I'm thinking in this moment is that when I get out of these bonds, I'm going to tear your arms and legs off, beat you over the head with them, and when I'm finished with that, I'm going to take that spray bottle and shove it right up your ass—the whole damn thing—and let's see how quickly you climax then." George was showing his teeth again.

"There's no need to be unpleasant." Ronald tugged at his lab coat. "I'm just doing my job. If you'd just cooperate—"

"No. You've failed at your job, so you might as well just un-tie me and then fucking run, and maybe I won't chase you down. I'll go looking for the nearest fucking exit instead. Deal?"

But no, Ronald was shaking his head. "I'm going to have to get the supervisor. He'll have to give you another jab to knock you out. I've never read of a shifter who prefers to climax in their sleep, but if that's what it takes—"

"If you or anyone else touches me in any way, I'll sue you, your department, your lab director, and anyone else connected with this godforsaken place until you're left panhandling on the side of the road. Do you hear me? I do not give my consent!"

"Things would go so much easier for you if you had," Ronald said sadly. "I don't know why they want your spunk so badly, but this is beyond my pay grade. I'd rest for a minute if I were you. The supervisor doesn't have my pleasant personality."

You won't have any personality left by the time I've finished with you, George grumped as Ronald left the room. *Come on, bear, fight, my furry friend. I need you free so we can get out of here. We have to get back to Scott.*

Chapter Twenty-One

Scott

Banging on Dakata's door, they did his best to stop the terror circulating through them, battering at the tiny thread of self-control he had left. All his life, Scott had no problem holding it together.

He had more than enough experience with his family to learn control. Yet, in this moment, he had none. It fled with the knowledge that someone had his blissful one and could do untold harm to him. He wanted his mate safe and in his arms. He didn't care how they had to achieve that, but it was all he could think about.

The door opened before he could bang again. Dakata appeared to tower over him with a pissed-off look Scott was more than familiar with, his demon side not so much, but they didn't care. "I need you to summon Merihem," his demon demanded without ceremony.

Dakata blinked slowly as he looked from Scott's demon to Dougal and back. "What's going on? And why would I be doing that?"

"We got a bit of a problem—"

"A bit of a problem!" he screeched at Dougal. "My mate has been abducted, and something is blocking our connection. Dougal believes it's his family, one I know nothing about. I don't even know what George's real name is." He threw up his arms. "How am I supposed to find him when I don't know where to start? I need your help, please," he begged around a harrowing sob.

"Let them in," Silas murmured from somewhere inside the house.

Dakata stepped aside, and only then did they notice he wore only boxer briefs, not that his demon was wearing anything.

Silas appeared, tying a long flowing robe at his middle that reached his bare feet. "Come sit, and I'll make some ginger and lemongrass tea."

The politeness of it all would have impressed Scott if not for their utter panic, which was coming from him and his demon, who was growing more fretful the longer he continued to search for their connection to George and couldn't find it.

"Explain what's going on," Dakata stated brusquely.

"George is missing. He didn't turn up to collect me from the office. My demon can't feel our connection to him. I came to the forest, because I knew this was where George heads when he needs some thinking time. When I realized something was wrong, I got Miller to bring me to the forest. He took me to the wrong place, then left after I expressly asked him to wait."

Dakata stared at him with such concern that Scott struggled to keep seated. "What do you mean? Miller left you in the woods and drove off? He has been my driver for twenty years, why would he do that? Why drop you in the wrong place? The man has an excellent sense of direction, so I don't get how he got you lost?"

"How would I know," he snapped, then took a deep breath that did fuck all to help. Each of Dakata's questions added a ball of anxiety to his stomach. As they developed, each one got bigger until the damn boulders were weighing Scott down. "I'm sorry," he muttered through clenched teeth when he got a narrow-eyed look from Dakata that was all warning.

His demon could barely move his legs as he rose off the couch, wanting to pace off the dread that grew with every passing second he waited for Merihem to arrive. "All I know is I asked him to take me where I thought George might be. After running about the damn forest attempting to find Dougal in the hopes that George would be with him, I got nowhere. So, I headed back to the car only to find it and Miller, gone."

"None of this makes sense," Dakata muttered as Silas came from the kitchen carrying a tray of drinks.

"It seems this Miller person is in cahoots with whoever took George," Dougal murmured, rubbing at his jaw while taking a mug from Silas.

"You think George being taken is a setup, and Miller aided in it?" Dakata didn't sound like he believed it.

Except why else would Miller drop Scott in the wrong part of the woods, ensuring that he delayed Scott? "This is all well and good, but we need Merihem and his skills to see if he can locate George for me."

Dakata went to a bowl near a window, and Scott saw him reach in and pull out several colored tumbling stones. His eyes closed, and Scott's nerves danced at each passing second Dakata stood motionless.

When he opened his eyes, his demon was there. "I've summoned him. Be patient, he is busy dealing with something else."

"Something else?" They weren't sure if the 'something else' was Peni, and if so, then he felt bad. If it was Merihem taking care of some person who had committed a heinous crime, then couldn't they wait? George was out there somewhere, enduring who knew what.

"He was working," Dakata supplied as if he had read their mind.

"Here, drink this, it will help settle you." Silas offered him a mug and a gentle smile.

Scott worked at putting a smile on his face when Dakata gave him another warning look that suggested snapping at Silas would be a mistake. He took the warm mug. "Thank you."

Dakata looked at Dougal, who had taken the seat Scott had vacated. "What do you know about George's family?"

Dougal was back to scratching at his jaw, his eyes on Scott. "George's father is the leader of a sleuth of bears that have strong lineage to some of the first ever bear shifters. Over the centuries, their lineage has become diminished through interbreeding. George, however, is a purebred.

"His father has definite ideas about how George should give up his sperm and create as many cubs as possible to keep the lineage going as the last true purebred bear of his fathers. A true sperm donor, if you will. George has other ideas about that and left the sleuth, changed his name, and has been in hiding ever since."

Scott's tea sloshed over the back of his hand, he didn't notice it burning his skin as he growled. "No one is having sex with my blissful one. No one!"

"What the hell is all this shouting about?" Merihem materialized in front of Dakata. Merihem wore trousers but nothing else in his demon form. Blood smeared his chest and dripped from the claws of one hand. "And why the urgency for me to finish with the asshat I was sending to hell?"

"We have a situation," Dakata supplied before Scott could gather his wits at the thought of George being forced to have sex with someone.

Scott didn't know how that was possible, as George had claimed Scott and he had touched George, making the blissful connection. He was pretty sure that would stop George from being able to get hard for anyone—*he hoped.*

"Someone has kidnapped George, it seems, and severed the connection to Scott." Dakata sounded so matter-of-fact it helped a little, but not much.

"Severed how? Drugs or..."

Scott wailed. "He's not dead. I would know," he insisted. "I would." His demon kept quiet.

"Drugs, I'd say. They gave him something when they took him to the hospital after the crash," Dougal supplied, watching them all with a look Scott couldn't even begin to fathom.

"That could be a problem..." Merihem gave Scott a searching look. "Can you feel anything? Sense his spirit?"

He couldn't speak for the lump in his throat, so he shook his head, blinking back the tears frantically clutching the mug.

"Fuck…" Merihem went to run his bloody hand through his hair, stopped and then dragged it down the leg of his trousers. "Come here, Scott. I need to touch you, get a sense of your connection to George."

Plonking the mug down on a small table, he went to Merihem and offered his hands. "No, I need to touch where George bit you?"

Naked after their rampage through the woods, they could see George's claim. Scott wasn't keen on Merihem touching it, but these were desperate times.

Merihem placed his still sticky fingers against the raised bite mark, his eyes flickered, changing color. Scott held his breath, wanting to get Merihem to rush, but also wanting him to find George.

"I can't get an exact location on him—"

"Fuck!" Scott bellowed at the crushing reality.

"Give me a fucking moment to finish. I can't get an exact location because of the corruption to your link, but I sense the area he's being held in. It'll be a mile or two radius from where George is."

Scott's legs wobbled, and he had to lock his knees to keep standing from the relief they had something to go on. "That's good."

We need to go now.

Don't even start with me.

"Let's go," Dakata stated, looking at Merihem.

Merihem smirked. "You might wanna put some pants on first."

Dakata snapped his fingers and was dressed a second later, wearing a scowl.

"I'll come, too," said Silas.

"What? Wait, no."

Silas didn't listen to Dakata and came to thread his arm through his, giving him a smile that clearly said he wasn't listening. "George might need my help."

Silas looked at Dougal. "Do you have some of your special brew?"

Dougal rooted about in a coat with numerous pockets and pulled out a flask.

"What's that?"

"It's a healing potion for animals," Dougal explained, giving it to Silas.

"Give it to me, I'll take it, and you can stay here."

Scott wanted to snap at Dakata for wasting time, but he got why he didn't want his blissful one coming into a dangerous situation with an unknown foe.

Silas tutted at Dakata. "I need my bow and arrows." One arched look, and Silas wore dark clothing, holding his bow and a shoulder harness holding arrows.

"If we're done with the arguing part of the evening, I have my own blissful one waiting at home, so shall we get on with this." Merihem took hold of Scott's hand and Dakata's, who had hold of Silas. The air shimmered around them, then they were deep in a forest that smelled of... chemicals.

His demon cast out, searching for George. His pulse was hammering hard enough to make it difficult to hear, they had to take three calming breaths to get to focus. There, under the other scents, was the barest hint of their blissful one. "I can scent George," he murmured as Merihem let him go.

"Which way?" Silas whispered, his eyes glowing in the darkness of the surrounding dense trees. "I can use the trees to guide us."

"It's coming from the right, through that big clump of trees." Keeping his voice low, his eyes adjusted to the darkness. The woods were too quiet. None of the night creatures made a noise and sent shivers of apprehension through Scott.

"Scott, walk at my side. I'll guide you."

There was a rumble of complaint from Dakata, but he said nothing as they set off. Each twig breaking set Scott's pulse to leap as they went deeper into the woods. The air wasn't fresh but stagnant beneath the chemicals.

Scott wasn't sure how long they walked through the woods before George's scent thickened the air. His teeth ground together, and his heart pounded hard enough to give him a headache. Because the scent didn't give Scott joy, it brought back the fear, because all he could smell was George's arousal. The scent was potent enough to make them react, and his demon's claws were ready to shred whoever thought they could touch their blissful one. His cock, hard and aroused to the point of pain, was just as ready to stab anything that got in its way.

"What the fuck," Merihem hissed in his ear. "Sexy time isn't on the fucking agenda here!"

Scott's demon glowered at Merihem, whether he could see it or not. "I fucking know that!" he ground out. "Someone has aroused my blissful one. I'm reacting to that, okay!"

An earth-rumbling roar filled the air and Scott's demon froze before he took off running. *I'm coming, my honey bear.*

I'm coming!

Chapter Twenty-Two

George

Shit was coming. George could smell it, although the scent of his own arousal was doing a damn good job of clogging up his nose. He'd never been disgusted by his cock before, but there had been something potent in that potion, and he was worried sick that it wouldn't go down until he'd found a release... somewhere... not in a damn lab with a man hovering with his pottle jar.

But no. Another smell was getting closer, one he knew from his nightmares. His father was a proud bear shifter, except he shunned ever smelling of an animal, and as the scent George could pick up got closer, he realized some things never changed, including his father's preferred cologne.

The footsteps coming down a hallway paused by the door, and a murmur of voices could be heard.

George scowled as he looked down at his naked body. *Vulnerability is a state of mind,* he reminded himself. He flexed his fingers. His bear was so close to breaking free, but he just wasn't there yet. Nothing would be able to hold him down if he could shift... *Keep working on it, bear. Keep pushing.*

The door swung open, and his father walked in alone, shaking his head in that condescending manner George remembered from when he was a kid. "You seem to be in a bit of a predicament." His father's sneer hadn't changed either, as he closed the door behind him.

"It's temporary." George's biceps bulged as he strained against the bonds.

"You've grown into a sizeable adult. I'm impressed." His father came closer, his dark hair cut in the same sharp style he'd always favored, and his suit still had that new clothes starchy smell.

"Did you think I was going to wither away outside of your influence?" George curled his lip. "I didn't need you or your name to do well for myself, *Cuthbert.*" He knew how much his father hated anyone using his first name.

"You consider driving a cab doing well for yourself?" Cuthbert's laugh was cruel, although George noticed it didn't bother him anymore. It confirmed to George the paramedic had to have been on his father's payroll and that people had been watching him all that time, not that it made any difference now. "As my son, I expected you to do so much better with your life."

"I'm content, Cuthbert. Can you say the same? I live by my rules, my way, and I don't have to kiss your ass for anything. Win-win in my opinion."

"And yet here you are, helpless, hanging onto the urge to orgasm to the point you're ready to scream with frustration."

George wanted to wipe that smug look off his father's face so badly that his fingers itched with it. "Is that what you think?" George flapped his useless hand, indicating the pristine lab. His bear was using his controlled anger to break the barrier between them, and George could sense it was working. He just needed a tiny bit more time.

"How much money did you spend on this latest whim of yours? Do your staff know that the moment they fail—which they have in this case—they'll be out on their ear without so much as a reference? Have you given them your patented lecture on how you can't abide failures?"

Cuthbert's grimace was all the answer George needed. "This lot would've cost you a pretty penny, and what did you get out of it? Some spunk from some non-consenting men who were used as guinea pigs." George laughed harshly. "Great. You've created your own spank bank. Just don't expect me to make a deposit."

"You want to."

Cuthbert's hand got closer to George's cock, and George growled. "You might've contributed to my genetics, but you don't own my cock or anything that comes out of it."

Cuthbert's hand moved away, and he folded his arms across his chest. "I don't understand why you have such an issue with all this. Your bloodline is special, pure, and deserves to be passed on to future generations."

"Who said?" George did the best he could to shrug, considering his restraints. "You? Tell me the same thing from someone whose opinion I actually give a fuck about because that's not you."

"You don't have to have anything to do with the cubs." Cuthbert threw up his hands. "You give a deposit and walk away. I swear on my bear I'll never contact you again."

"That might be how you do things, *except* it's not my way." George was seething. "I didn't even realize I had a father until I was ten years old, and you only came then because my mother was dying. You didn't give a shit about her. You definitely didn't give a shit about me, except as a commodity you could get mated off to one of your handpicked females who all follow you as if you're a god. If you're that bound and determined to have an heir who'll contribute their genetics to your gene pool, have another son. But wait. You can't, can you?"

George knew the barb hit home when his father's face became flushed. "I'm the only one, aren't I? How many girls came from your spunk? Everyone who can read knows it's the male of the species that contributes the X or Y chromosomes that determine gender. Your spunk is all about the girls. But hey, keep trying. You have got one son. Maybe in another fifty years, you'll have another one. In the meantime, you'd better let me go because if I have to get out of here under my steam, this place is going to be a mess."

"I'll let you go…" Cuthbert said slowly, a sly look on his face. "I'll let you go if you tell me why that potion, that, yes, I spent hundreds of thousands of dollars developing, didn't work on you."

George's eyes narrowed. His father never ever backed down. That was why George was strapped naked to a fucking metal table that they'd bolted to the floor. Cuthbert always got his own way, one way or the other.

"I did inherit something useful from you," he said, pushing at his bear with the last bit of energy he had left. "It's called willpower. My dick might be as hard as a fucking rock, and it makes no difference. That's biology. I'd rather piss on you than give you a single drop of my spunk. I won't have children carrying my genetics under your control. Period. End of fucking story."

"That stubbornness came from your mother." Cuthbert pulled a pair of latex gloves out of his jacket pocket and then went over to the door and George heard the lock click. A shiver ran down his spine.

"The things I have to do to get one simple bloody sample." Cuthbert pulled on his gloves, snapping the edges of them as he got closer. "I guess I'll have to do a spot of milking the bull, seeing as you're not in a position to give me a hand."

"You fucking touch me, and that's incest. You'll have to kill me to stop me shouting that story from the rooftops and spreading it across media outlets nationwide. I'll go to the Shifter Council, I'll have your picture plastered over every news outlet there is. Your reputation will be ruined. You'll become known as the man so desperate to control his only son, he sexually abused him—sexually abused your own son just to get your own way."

"You won't tell anybody." Cuthbert's sneer was calculating. "You'll be so ashamed when you slink out of here. You'll never speak of this again."

"I said *no*!" George bellowed, loud enough to raise the ceiling. His bear burst free, the straps fell from his body. A moment later, the door smashed open, and that's when all hell came for a visit.

Chapter Twenty-Three

Scott

His demon didn't hesitate, ramming at doors like they were twigs to get to where he could scent George. He heard Dakata and Merihem charging behind him, only they were way too incensed to consider waiting. The pheromones were doing a number on them. The fury was like nothing Scott had experienced—or allowed himself to release. Years of abuse from his family, fueled by his impotence to do anything to fight back, merged into a fire that lit his damn soul.

Through the locked door, naked, his hard cock bobbing madly in time to his pulse, his gaze swept the room, searching for their enemy. Their honey bear was there roaring his displeasure at the other suited man wearing black gloves. They matched in height and stature.

Despite the similarities to George, the other man's eyes held none of the warmth. "What did you do to my honey bear," his demon demanded in a tone that would slice off a person's balls.

"Who the fuck are you," the suited man fired back with fury.

The demon stepped around a roaring George and gripped the man by the throat, squeezing hard enough to make his eyes bulge from the sockets, he lifted him clear off the ground. He brought him closer, holding his hateful gaze. "Who am I?" he snarled. "I'm your worst fucking nightmare." He reached for the hand that balled to punch him, took hold of the wrist, and snapped it back.

"Arrrrggggggghhhhh," he scream—gurgled, spit sliding out his mouth as it gaped open when they squeezed harder.

They laughed in his face when the unbroken hand came up, scratching at the fist on his throat.

"Did you touch my blissful one?" he asked so quietly, yet the threat in the words was unmistakable. "Did you?"

When the man spat at him, his eyes shifting, his bear there ready to emerge, they lifted him higher and shook him violently, then threw him onto the table bolted to the ground. Quick as a flash, they flipped him onto his front, leaped up, and jumped on the center of his back. The weight effectively pinned the fucker to the table like they must have done to their blissful one. They grabbed a dangling strap and wrapped it around his neck, pulling back until he arched backward, choking and screaming.

Nothing satisfied them, when they didn't know who had dared to touch their bear. They got close to his ear. "Did you touch my blissful one? Get some of his spunk?"

A hand touched his arm, and his head fired around, ready to snarl, only to meet George's beautiful eyes. "Honey bear," he cried in relief, his hands relaxing.

"I'm here, my love. He got nothing from me. Nothing," he spat at the man they held fast. The hand pressed a little firmer, helping ground them when there was the connection they had lost.

"I'll… get… what I want in the end," howled the man beneath them. "It's my fucking DN… argggghhhh," he gargled as they tightened the strap, twisting so hard blood seeped past the leather.

Scott couldn't remember a time he wanted to kill another person as much as he did then. He, though more an observer in this, wanted exactly what his demon wanted. Blood. Death, to be inflicted painfully for daring to hurt George. "You will get fuck all," they roared, incensed once more. "He is my blissful one. My mate. You took him from me. You dared to lay hands on him when the universe has deemed him mine for eternity."

Merihem moved to the table. Blood remained on his chest, and his expression was that of evil incarnate, causing them a moment of wonder. Was this how Merihem looked when he went to dole out death? "I'll deal with him."

The gargling sounds coming from the man made no sense as he attempted to twist and wriggle away. The sound of shoes thudding down the hallway made them look up in time to see a man running past the doorway. "Dakata, stop him."

Dakata was already moving, and within a minute, had returned, gripping the other man by the back of his neck. "Now, where do you think you're going?" he growled fiendishly.

The guy immediately blubbered like a baby. "I didn't touch him."

"Who the fuck strapped me to the table?" George growled.

The upset was enough to get them to jump off the table in a fluid move, knowing Merihem would take over. They lifted George clear off the ground, hugging him tightly. Naked skin touching naked skin made them shudder and George groaned in that sexy way he did when he was getting ready to cum.

Scott grew conflicted by the arousal and the audience, his demon had no such issue. He was not stopping. The feel of George's pre-cum rubbing up their belly as he wrapped his legs around their hips and rutted against them, increasing the smell of arousal. It enticed them into madness.

"Scott, be sensible, you don't want any of George's cum left in here."

Dakata's words sank past the lust, and Scott didn't give his demon a chance to protest and translocated them back to George's home. Scott didn't think about why he felt this was better for both of them when there was another priority. Reaffirming their connection.

His demon didn't relinquish his form. A need Scott could not deny him when George's hot mouth moved down their throat, kissing and nibbling, leaving a trail of delicious sensations that made them throb with untold need.

The two sides warred. Scott wanted to treasure George, yet with each inhale, his scent clouded Scott's demon's reasoning and made it harder to consider taking it slow.

"Don't want slow," George murmured hotly against his flesh, as if he had plucked the thought from their head. His teeth sank into their mating mark, sucking deep.

Their cock jerked against George's, cum painting his cock, marking him, covering the other chemical scents marring his skin. "That's it, come all over me," he rasped, releasing his bite to lick and murmur, "I'm yours, only yours. No one can have any part of me, because it belongs to you."

The words were heady after the emotional rollercoaster they had ridden. "Mine," his demon growled. "Forever."

"Forever," George replied, his mouth claiming theirs in a blistering kiss that easily brought back the ache of arousal.

Needing something more, his demon hiked George a little higher, holding him one-handed and with a thought, he conjured a bottle of lube.

What are you doing?

What does it look like? His demon's reply came with a dose of 'are you stupid'.

We don't—

You don't. I do. I want this, and so does our bear.

I'm not sure.

I am.

As if to prove his point, they pushed George up against the first flat surface, a door, and his demon, with another thought, de-clawed his fingers and had lube on them.

George growled and moaned at once at the first touch to the crease of his ass when the insistent finger slid between his parted cheeks. The kiss became wild, and Scott had no other choice but to let go and sink into the madness that followed.

George made noises, none of which suggested they should stop. His demon twirled the tip of his lube finger over George's hole in teasing, gentle strokes, warming the sensitive flesh until George was rocking into each touch, encouraging them to continue.

When he pushed the tip of his finger into the clenching channel, they nearly came imaging how tight it would feel around their cock.

His mouth was released, and Scott expected George to draw things to a halt, convinced his blissful one would not be interested in what his demon side wanted. Their gazes locked and there was hunger. One that suggested that stopping right then was not up for discussion.

The tension built between them as the sound of their ragged breathing filled the quiet. "I want you," George exclaimed. "I want all of you. Will you give it to me?"

Scott understood George was speaking to him in that moment. "We will. He understands now you are all that is important to us. Nothing else matters."

Amusement lit George's eyes. "Never thought I'd be grateful to dear old dad for anything." His mouth landed back on theirs, and any thoughts on the subject fled.

Somewhere along the way, they found their way to the bed, and George rode three fat fingers, begging for more in such a way that they struggled not to come from the luscious sight he made beneath them.

The bed creaked ominously as George rolled them so fast, they landed on their back with him above, straddling them. His eyes gleamed with a dark passion that left them breathless and yearning for him to take charge.

When he reached back and took hold of their cock, they groaned in approval. He sank down, inch by delightful inch. His body glistened with sweat as they rode the intense pleasure, sharing it through their bond. It was there, glowing between them, in them, making the universe become just about them. Every muscle in their bodies slowly filled with a pleasure like no other. It made everything else inconsequential. There was just this. Just them.

They gasped together, opening their souls. The beauty of sensuality came with each roll of George's hips as he rocked, keeping their cock deep inside him, like he couldn't bear to let go. Heat, unimaginable, searing hotness, traveled from their cock to their balls and up the spine to zap at any and all of Scott's brain cells, working to derail each and every one, rendering them useless.

George topped from the bottom, giving him a sexy fucking grin that melted his heart and made his cock so hard it felt like it might burst when his large hands landed on their chest. "Ready for the ride of your life?" his bear growled, pinning him to the bed.

"Yes," he moaned breathlessly. "Yes, fuck yes."

Chapter Twenty-Four

George

Never in his life would he have thought he'd have a cock up his ass, except right now, it was all he wanted. The pale blue demon was stunning, and a temptation George had never considered. With whatever potion his father had gotten the dickweed to make and spray on him, he had needs that left him here, sitting on his demon's cock and fucking loving it.

If he was going to have a meltdown about that, it sure as hell wasn't now when this mate was moaning "yes" in that sassy, demanding voice that was part Scott, part demon. Something else that was irresistible.

The pole in his ass lit fires that trailed a blaze from the soles of his feet to the end of every strand of hair on his head as he rocked his hips. He ground down when Scott hit a spot that made him leak all over the pale blue skin, making it glisten in the overhead lights that had gotten flicked on when they had bounced off the switch coming through the door.

On and on, he rocked and moaned in time with Scott. It was as if he was being taken apart and being put back together. Only this time, the pieces fit perfectly with Scott's. "That's it. Show me how much you want me."

He shivered and moaned. "I do, my honey bear. I want you to come all over me."

George's cock hurt with the need to come, yet he wanted his demon to come first. He needed it more than food, air, and water. Combined. He squeezed and rocked. "Then come for me. Fill me until all I smell of is you."

The light caught the delicate blue of their demon's neck as he arched, his hands clasping George's hip bones hard enough to mark, whimpering, "Fuck, yes."

His face was an exquisite mask of pain and pleasure, one George could not look away from. His own arousal pulsed as the one in his ass expanded further before warmth spread deep inside him.

"I'm comingggg," his demon howled.

George's cock erupted hard, a volcano couldn't have spurted with more intensity. Cum sprayed pale blue skin, the headboard of the bed, and the wall behind it as George's balls throbbed and gave up a gallon of cum. Minutes passed as he decorated his demon, who made an erotic picture, rubbing cum into his skin with one hand while gathering and licking cum off the other. "So yummy," he groaned around the fingers in his mouth.

A sexy ass move that ensured George kept on coming until he collapsed, exhausted long minutes later. He lay there on top of his mate, who clasped him tightly to his body, appearing unwilling to let go, which was fine with George, despite feeling a little uncomfortable with the remaining semi-hard cock in his ass.

Listening to the heart slow beneath his ear, George drifted on the spent euphoria of the most epic orgasm of his life. His eyes shutting, he snuggled in.

Okay.

Well.

That happened. George had woken in his own bed, which was fabulous, curled around Scott, who'd shifted back to his human form sometime in the night. There wasn't any stickiness anywhere, so Scott's demon must've cleaned them at some point, which was sweet, but the air still held the lingering traces of their climaxes.

This is home… the way my home was meant to be. My mate in my arms, my bed smelling of our delicious, combined scents. George closed his eyes and just savored the moment.

Would I be the asshole if I hoped Scott sleeps for the next two or three days just so we can enjoy this?

George's eyes didn't stay closed for long. Scott, when he wasn't tensed up, when he wasn't anxious, when he was just sprawled across George's sheets without a care in the world, was the most beautiful sight in existence. George defied anyone to tell him otherwise.

Musing about how he wished Scott would trust him enough to let go of his tight controls at times, it was only natural for his brain to wander over the events of the past day—two days—George had no idea. In captivity and away from Scott, it was easy to imagine every minute was a lifetime, and it wasn't as though George had a watch or a phone handy. *Shit. They're going to have to be replaced... assholes.*

In a weird, backhanded way, George was relieved his father had finally made his move. After having spent most of his life always looking over his shoulder, being so careful about who had his information and why, changing his whole identity, and living as far under the radar as he could... *I should've known good old Cuthbert would find me, eventually.*

Not that it had done Cuthbert any good. George had no doubt Merihem and Dakata would take care of him, making sure no one would find the remains. He wouldn't be surprised if he read in the news about a giant fire somewhere remote, either. At the end of the day, it didn't matter. Cuthbert had played his last hand and lost.

George's heart rate increased as he thought about how close he'd come to being violated. Cuthbert's hand hovering so close to his dick. Scott stirred and murmured something, and George held his breath, trying to control his emotions.

It's over.

It's over.

It's over! His bear had come through. Scott had smashed his way into the lab and brought friends. Cuthbert was never going to bother him again. *Everything is going to be all right.*

I hope.

Smiling ruefully in the dim light, George shook his head. When he and his mate were naked together, they fit with each other effortlessly. George would never know if it was his father's potion that spurred him into giving up his ass for his demon, or if it was something else. Some deep, hidden desire he had and just hadn't acted on before, perhaps. It didn't matter. It was done. George wasn't sure if he'd do it again, but he wasn't going to have a conniption about it. He'd been willing, it was fun… *But sooner or later, Scott is going to pull on a suit again and…*

They were going to have to talk. George knew it. Scott probably did, too. After all, his mate was an intelligent man. Casting his eyes around the room, George inhaled sharply before letting it out slowly. *I'm not in danger anymore,* which had been Scott's excuse for wanting to stay at his sterile penthouse. Now, all George had to do was get his mate to stop working for five minutes so they could sit down and have a solid heart-to-heart. And if that talk included Scott recognizing George's house as a possible home...

Don't go getting ahead of yourself. George didn't know what had happened to his brand-new taxi. Was it stuck in that non-existent road where he'd been taken, or had the guy who took him used it to get them to wherever his father's lab had been? Was driving a cab even a good idea when all he wanted was to be with Scott while the man was working? Questions, questions, questions.

Enjoy the moment, his bear suggested, and that was good advice. Tucking Scott under his arm, George closed his eyes and let sleep take him.

Chapter Twenty-Five

George

It wasn't often that George got out of bed before his lovely demon, but Scott was still sleeping soundly when he slipped out, took a quick shower, and then went to inspect the contents of his refrigerator. There wasn't a lot there—basically because he'd spent most of his time since meeting his mate at Scott's place. But a quick trip to the corner store just down the road, and George had the fixings for a decent breakfast. He'd also bought buns in case

Scott got up and immediately wanted to get to the office. At least George could take solace in that he'd sent Scott off with a meal.

When Scott stumbled in twenty minutes later, he didn't seem to be dressed for the office. He wasn't dressed at all. He had one of George's comforters wrapped around him, with just his head sticking out. His hair was still all over the place, and George smiled widely.

"You're just in time for breakfast. Did you sleep well?" He wanted to say something about "ignore the mess," but he didn't want to attract Scott's attention to his everyday clutter.

"Hugs first." Scott shuffled around the counter as George hurriedly shoved the fry pan off the heat. "I woke up, and you weren't there."

"You had a busy day yesterday. I wanted to provide you with some sustenance." George pulled Scott into his arms. "Demon heroes who double as busy executives need their food."

"Merihem won't let me into the office." Scott yawned. He didn't seem upset about it. "Him and Dakata want to see us in the forest this afternoon. By the way, Merihem found your taxi. That's being delivered here in about an hour."

"For someone so sleepy, you still manage to get a lot done," George teased, dropping a kiss on Scott's mussed hair before taking a longer smooch when Scott tilted up his face. "We don't want the eggs to go rubbery, babe," he added when they finally pulled apart. "Have a seat. I'll bring you a plate."

"I love this." Scott must've still been half asleep because he shuffled back around the counter and dropped into the nearest chair, pushing aside a pile of mail George had left there. "Your place is so much more homely than mine. I don't think I've ever slept so well and every room smells... amazing." He blushed a bright pink, like he'd just realized what he'd said aloud.

"That could be the bacon you're smelling." George quickly served up the food onto two plates. *Don't get your hopes up.* "Here," he added as he came around the counter with the plates, putting them on the table. "Eat this, and you'll feel more like yourself."

"I don't want to feel like my other self. I want to feel like this. Warm. Comfortable. Loved." Scott picked up a knife and fork and looked George right in the face. "I think I need help with that."

Suppressing his happy dancing bear wasn't easy, but George managed to confine his glee to a wide smile. "Then

you're in the right place. Eat first, babe, and then tell me
how I can help."

Scott

He meant it. He would need help, maybe. The fear had
driven out all of his old behaviors because nothing was as
important as George's safety to him. They had expressed
that repeatedly over night. Scott had let his demon have
his way, and he'd let him have his way again if George got
to moaning the way he did when…

His demon was laying back once more, fanning himself,
utterly smug about his conquest of their blissful one.

He loved it.

*Maybe, but don't get your hopes up that he'll want to do it
again.*

*You leave that to me. You just keep with this relaxed, no fuss
pot vibe going and we'll be all good.*

Scott rolled his eyes at his demon and munched on the
crispy bacon his stomach demanded. It was the smell, and
the lack of a warm body pressed against his that brought

Scott out of the bedroom. He'd grabbed the nearest thing to hand to wrap around his body—it smelled of George. It comforted him, which he and his demon half were still in need of. The text he had gotten from Merihem telling him to take a few days off left him not in the least bit conflicted.

Leaving George, no, he wasn't ready for that when he did not know if the threat to George was definitely over. The message said little, only requesting them to pay a visit to the forest later today, with George.

There was also the issue of whether George would be upset about whatever Merihem and Dakata did to the great buffoon.

Asshole. Fucktard. Shit head. These are more like it.

Yes, well, that may be the case, but we don't want to upset George. He's suffered enough.

"Is there a reason you're scowlin' at the bacon?" George asked, a worried furrow appearing as he eyed Scott's plate.

"I…" Scott sighed, and he caught George tensing. "Your father…" he held George's gaze. "Will you be upset if they—"

"Got rid of his superior attitude about what he can and can't have that belongs to me?" He shook his head. "I've spent years hiding, worrying about when he'd finally catch up with me." A black look appeared, one Scott had never witnessed before. "The fucker was gonna milk me like a cow."

Scott pushed back from the table, body shuddering with outrage. The comforter fell to the floor as he glowered. "He was going to do what!" he bellowed, his demon ready to emerge and hunt the fucker down and chop off his hands—even though that had probably already been done.

George chuckled and placed his cutlery down, pushed back his chair, and patted his lap.

They didn't need words, Scott was on his lap in a heartbeat.

George held him close, his nose nuzzling into Scott's hair. "You saved me." Those three words swept away the anger, and Scott's body responded to the bulge growing under his ass.

He lifted up for a kiss and wasn't disappointed when George gave him one that curled his bare toes and left another part of him straining for attention.

Somehow or other, sometime later, Scott was sweaty and sticky, lying in the center of George's enormous bed with his blissful one, breathing hard and pinning him to the covers.

He grinned up at the ceiling, not feeling in the least bit guilty about the fact George had... ravished him, "On a workday," he giggled.

George shifted and rolled, bringing Scott with him to settle on top of him. "Workday?"

Scott blushed, or he probably would have if he wasn't already flushed from their make-out session. "Doing this"—he pointed between them—"during work hours. A workday."

The hand stroking down towards his ass paused, and back was the tension filling George's body. "Is that a problem?"

Nothing about the tone suggested George was worried, but through their connection, Scott felt it. He understood his past behavior, which he'd already said he'd need help with from George, was to blame. He made himself a little more comfortable, lying fully on George, folding his arms on top of George's chest so he could rest his chin on them and meet his gaze. "I have OCD, I know I do, and by acting the way I have, I've made you feel..."

"Worried I'm not enough for you," George whispered.

Scott accepted the stab of sorrow at the words because they were the truth. "I felt like I was the one not good enough for you. That because I'm different, 'not perfect' that I needed everything around me to be perfect when I'm not."

George's growl was all threat. "Your family's got a lot to answer for. There is nothing wrong with you." He slipped his hands under Scott's armpits and dragged him up his body until their lips were nearly touching. The skin sliding against skin got a groan from both men, but George never wavered. "No one is perfect, not a soul alive. Me and my bear, we want you here in our home. Want you to make a home with us. We don't care about whether or not your behavior is perfect. Whether the house has a little clutter here and there. None of that matters 'cause we have you."

Scott gave a very undignified sniff and did his best to blink back the tears stinging his eyes at the sincerity of his bear's words. "I want to promise that stuff won't make me want to tidy and clean, because we know I'd be lying. But you might want to offer... a reward system to me to distract me." As Scott said it, he and his demon warmed to the idea.

Sexual rewards.

Behave.

Hell no. I might even encourage you to go all fuss pot for sex.

"Reward system?"

"Yep. Say I have a bad day and I'm annoying you with my behavior, you offer me a reward. We could make a chart where I get to pick something."

George's smile was so wide it nearly stretched to his ears. "This I can totally get on board with." He rolled them once more, his arousal digging into Scott's hip. "So, what do you have in mind to put on the list?"

"Snuggling with your bear," his demon said for Scott.

The light in his eyes made Scott melt with the warmth. "My bear would be very agreeable to that." He rubbed his nose down Scott's, kissing him softly. "What else?"

~/~/~/~

Scott carried in two of the suitcases he had packed in his *old* home and brought them into George's house. His blissful one was behind him, hefting the other two. "How many suits did you cram in here? And how the heck do they weigh so much?"

The grumble was all amusement, and Scott fired a grin over his shoulder at the man who had had a lot of fun in creating a reward list to distract Scott when his need for control got out of hand. "You have my shoes, not the suits."

"Shoes, suits, they still weigh a ton."

"I just brought as much as I think I'll need," he replied, placing the suitcases in the spare bedroom that had a big, empty closet that was going to be Scott's. The room had a set of drawers and a very comfy-looking armchair that would work for an office seat.

"I can't see anyone needing twenty suits," George muttered good-naturedly as he placed them carefully next to the other ones. "You look good wrapped in my comforter or..." his gaze became heavy lidded, and a flare of desire appeared in the depth of his eyes, "naked."

"I've created a monster," Scott stated, lifting his hands to ward off the man coming towards him. "We have to go, head to the forest. We don't want to be late."

Are you sure? Look how cute our honey bear is with a pout.

His big shoulders shrugged, his jacket tightening around a bicep as he ran a hand through his messy hair. And pouting as his demon pointed out. "We could go tomorrow?"

At how hopeful he looked, Scott wanted to give in. Only his innate sense of work ethic and the hate of letting people down, had him shaking his head. "Dakata is still my boss. And as much as I want to stay and..." he waited for a beat, "unpack."

George snorted and reached into his pocket. Cell phone in hand, his eyes alight, he tapped at the screen. "Reward, pick one."

Sneaky. You did that on purpose. His demon sounded shocked.

So what?

I like it.

Scott huffed and came forward to look at the screen. "I'll take the back rub. After lifting those suitcases, I could do with one."

George gave him a suspicious look. "You did that on purpose," he accused.

Scott kissed his once more pouting lips. "Who me? Never." He gave him a saucy smile. "The quicker we get to the forest, the quicker we get to come home."

George's face transformed into a stunning smile. "I like how that sounds."

"Getting back quicker?"

"No, that you see this as your home."

Heart trembling at the emotion George conveyed as their gazes held. Scott cupped George's cheeks and kissed him softly. "Any place with you in it is my home. The walls don't matter, it's the contents that do."

The kiss held a dreamy quality as they lingered, holding each other.

When George pulled back, he reached for Scott's hand. "Ready?"

Scott wasn't sure he was when it meant that work would once more come between them. "As I'll ever be."

Chapter Twenty-Six

George

The forest had been George's place of refuge from the first week he'd moved into town. Already tired from always looking over his shoulder, and still reeling from the last Cuthbert incident, when he'd bumped into Dougal that first time, while in his bear form, he felt accepted—as if he could truly be who he was in every way. That acceptance went a long way toward keeping George in town, even before he knew about Scott, even when he started to notice little things that indicated his father was getting close again.

So, when Scott translocated them to the clearing where he'd spent many a night drinking and chatting with the forest dwellers, George had no reason to feel uncomfortable or unsettled in any way. He found a log to sit on, encouraging Scott to sit on his lap. "So, your butt doesn't get grubby," he whispered when Scott seemed unsure, then nodded at the other people in the clearing.

Dakata was there with Silas on his lap. Merihem had his mate Peni on his lap, too. And Dougal, who never had anyone sitting on his lap but who waved his mug of cider in greeting. "I'm just here for moral support and to make sure your ugly mug was still intact," he said with a grin.

Dougal was good like that. "How's Wanda doing?" George asked, purely because he realized, seeing the gathering, that he hadn't seen her since she'd gone through her own trauma.

A strange look flashed over Dougal's face, but it was gone before George recognized what it was. "She's doing fine. She's got plenty of support around her... so yeah. Suffice to say, she's okay."

"I'm glad." George nodded. "Let me know if she needs anything from town." He looked around the gathering. "What's up?"

"You wanted to see us?" Scott had enough apprehension for both of them. "Am I going to lose my job?"

Really? Scott's worried about that?

But Dakata was shaking his head already. "That business would fall to pieces without you, and don't take that as a compliment, because it's a damn fact. So, you ran off to save your blissful one? It's done. Over. No one will discuss it again after this meeting, if that's your wish."

"I told you to take time off," Merihem added, "because you and your blissful one have gone through a very stressful time, and our blissful ones—Silas and Peni—have both said you need to spend time together to connect and feel…" he looked down at Peni who was grinning. "What's the word again?"

"You did fine with mentioning the connection aspects. Shifters who go through difficult times, and demons, too, need to spend time reconnecting. We've been through that ourselves, so you know what I mean." Peni was stroking Merihem's chest, and George would swear that the demon was purring, but what would he know?

"Right, so no more talk about being fired or leaving your job or stuff like that, Scott," Dakata said abruptly. "No, we have to talk about Cuthbert and Miller. Cuthbert is no more. Is that going to be a problem?"

George realized Dakata was talking to him directly. "I can't think why it would be. I'm sure Scott will be happier knowing I'm not under threat of being abducted again. I don't need to know what happened to him, just that he can't come back."

"He can't." Merihem looked grim. "But there is the little matter of the fact Cuthbert was running a clan, most of whom are related to you, and who see you as the heir of his estate and fortune, which is considerable even in demon terms. You are, or were, his only son."

"No, I'm not—his heir, I mean," George said quickly as Scott stiffened in his arms. "I went through a lawyer years ago, giving up my right to any of my father's businesses or estate. I thought it would get him to leave me alone. Besides," he added with a quick grin at his mate. "I wasn't always a taxi driver, and I do have enough investments of my own to keep my mate in chocolates and fluffy rugs if he ever wants to give up work."

"As if!" Dakata and Merihem roared with laughter.

George felt Scott's discomfort, only before he could say anything, both demons received slaps on their arms.

"You're not being nice," Silas glared at Dakata.

"And you'll be in big doo-doo if Scott decides to become a man of leisure," Peni added staunchly to Merihem. "Don't make fun of his hard work when it allows you to sit on your butts all day."

"Yeah. What he said." Dougal raised his mug. "No teasing the pretty blue demon. You're far nicer to look at in your demon form than the other two, Scott, so just ignore them."

"Thank you." Scott ducked his head. "Speaking of work, what's all this about Miller? Did he explain why he took me to the wrong place in the forest and just left me there?"

"Miller is a lying piece of shit!" Dakata shook his head in disgust. "He's worked for me for fucking years, and he threw it all away because of that Cuthbert idiot."

"What do you mean?" George tightened his hold on Scott as his mate looked at him in alarm. "There's no way Cuthbert would've connected Scott to me. We've not known each other that long."

"That might have been partially my fault," Merihem said. "I sent Scott to check up on you when you were in the hospital, remember?"

"That's when we met." Scott had such a pretty blush.

"Miller was driving you, and…" Merihem broke off.

George wasn't sure what he was going on about, but Scott's blush deepened.

"I demoned out," Scott whispered. "When I couldn't find you in the hospital, my demon was upset. Miller saw that."

"I'm still not seeing the connection between your driver and my father," George said, quietly pleased his mate had such a powerful reaction at the hospital. "It's not like the driver could know Scott and I were fated."

"No, but Miller was already working for your father," Dakata said grimly. "Cuthbert knew, don't ask me how because it's not like we can question him now, but he knew you came to the forest a lot, George. The only other car that came here was mine—"

"But that's not right," Silas interrupted. "We continued using George to transport us after you and I met because we didn't want anyone in your office to know where my tree was. Merihem and Peni used to call George too until the accident."

"And that accident had nothing to do with George's father," Peni added. "That was all that horrible demon with his maniacal laugh. I know he's not laughing now."

"Cuthbert had a finger in a lot of pies," Dakata said. "While the car accident was the fault of a different demon, the events afterward had Cuthbert's sticky fingers all over it, from insisting you got taken to the hospital, through to contacting Miller to monitor what happened from our company's side of things. I don't think he knew about the mate bond, but he knew there was something connecting my staff, the forest, and you."

"From what we heard in the lab—which made a lovely bonfire, thank you for asking—before the fire, we found out that George's DNA was meant to be collected at the hospital." Merihem wrinkled his nose. "You were right about that, George. It was perfect timing, as far as Cuthbert was concerned. You had a head injury, and then you got drugged by some idiot who didn't know better. That freaky potion would work on unconscious subjects. The hospital was desperately busy at the time, and by the time the lab got word that George was in the hospital, you'd already left."

"There's still some gaps in the story," Dakata admitted. "Cuthbert has been working behind the scenes in this town for years, by the looks of things. To know my fucking driver could be paid off so easily... it's not like I didn't pay him well because I did."

"Cuthbert had a way of making people feel special or valued," George said, still trying to get all the pieces in his head to fit. Then he realized what he'd said, and he looked up. "Not that you didn't," he added quickly. "It's just—"

"No. I know." Dakata still had a disgruntled look on his face. "Except, now I have to get a new driver..."

"George," Scott said suddenly.

"Yes, babe?"

"No, no, Dakata. George. Why not use George as your company driver?"

"Wait. What?" *Did Scott just volunteer me for a job?*

"The job pays really well, and you know about the forest and how to keep Silas's tree a secret because you do it already." Scott was speaking in a rush, as if he was worried the older demons would shut him down. "You'd get to spend time in the office with me, and while yes, you'll have to ferry the other demons around sometimes, they have their own drivers, or they translocate, so it would mostly be Merihem and me. The company car has heated seats and sat-nav and all that other technical stuff..." he trailed off, looking between George and Dakata. "I think it would be a good idea."

George couldn't stand seeing Scott look so indecisive. "Tell me where to send my resume," he said with an easy grin and a wink at his mate. "You can set me up with a comfortable chair in your office while I'm waiting for work."

"I haven't got the time to read your resume." Dakata snorted. "You're hired. You start next Monday when Scott goes back to work. Scott can draw up your contract and let you know about the pay and benefits. Agreed?"

"Would you be happy with this?" George kept his voice low, needing to know despite Scott being the one to suggest it. Sure, the others could probably hear him, but in that moment, he was focused on Scott alone.

Scott was biting his bottom lip as he nodded. "I'll live in your house, and you'll work at my work. We can be together. I think that would be… helpful."

Looking over Scott's head, George grinned at Dakata. "You've got yourself a driver. Just don't expect me to wear a suit to work. Now, if you don't mind, Scott and I need to discuss a few things between ourselves, so if there's nothing else?"

He was still grinning when Scott translocated them back to George's house. Their house now.

Chapter Twenty-Seven

Scott

Scott wasn't sure where he got the audacity to suggest that George be the company driver for him, except when the idea popped into his head, he felt it was the right decision.

George's simple acceptance made returning to the house a little less nerve-racking. Because now came the actuality of settling into George's home...

"You're back to frowning. What is it?" George asked, taking hold of Scott's hand to bring them to the couch. He threw a couple of cushions onto the other seat, and Scott watched them land and one topple to the floor.

Did his fingers itch to pick it up? Yes. All it took was one look at George's neutral expression to see that he was waiting for Scott to decide to stop him. "I know you're waiting for me to start fussing."

George plonked himself down on the couch and brought Scott with him, settling him on his lap like he'd done in the forest to stop his pants from getting dirty. It was the little things that mattered.

"I want you to relax," he spoke carefully, like he was picking his words. "And the reward system can help. I see that..."

"Except you want me to understand that the things that trigger me aren't an issue with you?" Scott finished off. "That when I start tidying, I make you feel uncomfortable, and I'm not thinking about you."

George's smile was as gentle as the finger he traced down Scott's cheek. "Yes. Its gotta be mighty hard to live up to all those expectations you got going inside"—he tapped the side of Scott's head—"of here."

Scott released a shuddery breath. "I think about you all the time. Then I think I'm going to be too clingy, and you'll hate it. When you came to work late the first time, I didn't say anything because of those very fears. Then you came with a fresh shirt on, clearly having gone home to shower, and I could see you didn't like being in my apartment."

"It's not that I don't like your apartment, I just worried I was gonna make a mess, and it would upset you."

Scott sighed and pressed his cheek against George's. "The little things, they creep up on me and then they become these big things, and I can't seem to stop them chasing me."

"Then what say we chase them together?" George moved beneath him and hugged him tighter. "Talkin', it's the only way to sort out things."

"So, I'll tell you when something is bothering me, and you won't be cross with me?" He sounded pathetic, except this was important. His family had always shut him down, and it had become a habit to keep his thoughts to himself. He needed to break free of old habits.

George growled. "I'll say it again, your family has got a lot to answer for." He kissed Scott on the cheek. "Yep, I want you to talk about whatever is on your mind."

The sincerity was genuine and unraveled the knots in his belly. "Maybe it's time I told my parents how they made me feel." As he said it, Scott understood that if he was ever really going to move forward, then he needed to offload the burden of his past.

"If you feel that's the right thing to do, then I'll support you."

You're going to go and tell them how you feel, good luck with that.

Not helping.

They showed us nothing but contempt.

Yes, and it's time they know we aren't putting up with that any longer.

Scott met George's gaze. "I do. Only I think I need to do it now, otherwise…"

"Let's eat before we go, so they don't spoil our appetite."

Scott chuckled at how serious George was. He shuffled off his lap and stood. "What do you fancy?" It was easier to keep his attention on a task rather than think about what he was going to say to his parents.

"Homemade patties, mushrooms, onions, and heaps of cheese, maybe a few fries." George got up and followed him. "I did a grocery shop this morning so we should have everything we need."

They worked together, and Scott liked the rhythm of it. He cleaned up as they went, but it wasn't manic. George talked about the contract Scott would draw up and the benefits, and by the time they sat to eat, Scott didn't bother to clear off the clutter on the table.

The atmosphere was much like it had been at breakfast, and it stopped the nervous anxiety Scott lived with constantly. George's presence, when he allowed it, soothed him. His bear was easy going.

When George took his plate and glass to the sink, Scott followed in companionable silence as they finished the cleanup.

George took the dishtowel from Scott's hands after he twisted it for the third time. "We don't have to go—"

He shook his head. "No, I do." He rolled his shoulders and reached for George's hand. "Don't let go."

"Never," George answered, squeezing his fingers.

In a blink, they were in Scott's bedroom—storeroom, and he didn't so much as glance about to see what else they had shoved in there. No, he was done worrying about the disrespect. He opened the door and listened out, then followed the sounds of voices. Only there was a voice he wasn't expecting to hear that drove him to quicken his pace. What the hell was the king doing here?

Fuck, had his parents followed through on their threats?

"What is it?" George whispered.

"The king is here!" he hissed back, hurrying. "They better not be trying to separate us." Fury, the kind that he'd felt at George's disappearance, came and fueled the need to stop his parents.

He more dragged than walked George into the large room his parents used for visitors. It was pretentious and ostentatious. Gold and red were the color theme, his father's attempt to mimic that of the throne room the demon king had. It looked like someone had vomited gold and red all over the room in a nasty pattern.

Asmodeus sat on an ornate chair his father liked to use. His face revealed none of his thoughts as he glanced at Scott while his parents, sitting on the most uncomfortable couch, failed to notice his arrival.

"I mean, it's an impossible situation. A bear, of all things,"—his father shuddered—"it'll bring disgrace on to our name. There must be something you can—"

"How dare you," Scott said with barely controlled rage at what he was hearing. "The disgrace is you, not George. He is my blissful one."

His parents' heads turned in his direction and Scott could see the disdain and disappointment—the two things he'd lived with his whole life. No more. George gave him courage and unconditional love, he needed nothing else.

"See, the boy, he's under the influence of that… creature," his father spat out. "Scott would never speak to us like that."

Scott came forward, George's fingers clasping his, helping him to focus. "Because I was always shut down. Made to feel less. Like I had nothing of value to contribute when I didn't look the same."

His father got up with an ugly sneer aimed at George. "We will talk about this when you can be civilized, and that creature isn't with you."

Scott let go of George and grabbed his father by the lapels of his very expensive suit, dragging him so close he could smell the wine he'd had with his supper. His demon side watched quietly, not intervening… *yet*. "You listen to me. I'm done being civilized. My blissful one is worth ten of you." His fists clenched tighter in the silk material as he yanked him still closer until their noses were nearly touching. He held his stare, seeing his father's eyes widen with shock. "Fate gave me a gift, despite what you believe, and I am worthy of it." He felt it deep in his core. George's love came through their bond, driving him on. "I am worthy of my honey bear. Nothing will change that." He glanced at Asmodeus. "Nothing. I will fight whoever tries to prove differently, and I will fucking win, you hear?" he demanded, his demon coming to the fore, uncaring that the demon king could tear them to pieces, not when it came to George.

Asmodeus rose, towering over them, fathomless dark eyes assessed him. "Have you finished?"

Scott released his father, making him stagger back and have to jerk to right himself or fall over. His mother then rose and went to him. The pair stared at him like they'd never seen him before. They hadn't, because they'd never seen who he was.

"Yes," he answered with a more civil tongue as George came and tugged Scott into his side in a protective move that set Scott's pulse thumping for a whole different reason.

"To be clear, you arranged for me to come to *your* home, so that you could complain about your son's choice of blissful one? That you wish for me to undo what Fate has chosen to give to Scott? Is that correct?"

Iciness dripped from each word and the hairs over Scott's body stiffened like an icy spray had blasted them. Tension radiated off George, who never took his gaze off Asmodeus.

"Why yes, it needs to be sorted," his father answered with probably a little too much condescension than he should have when aimed at Asmodeus. His mother nodded, offering a vapid smile.

"Nothing needs sorting, we're mated. You ain't changin' that."

Asmodeus gave George a fleeting look that Scott thought was all respect and something else, regret. "On that, we agree." He reached out a clawed hand and placed it against Scott's shirt. "Fate has spoken."

The hand fell away, and Scott got a weird feeling coursing through him. Had the king done something to him? He glanced at George, unsure what to make of it all.

George shrugged, but a gleam of amusement appeared in the depth of his gaze when he turned his attention to those in the room watching them wearing matching expressions of doubt. "We done?"

"I—"

Asmodeus gave his father a withering look that shut him up. "For now," he replied when looking at George.

George nodded. "Good, let's go home."

Scott gave his parents one last look. "If you ever find the part of decency—of love—that was missing when it comes to me, and now to my blissful one, you know where I work. Until that time, I won't be back." As he left, a part of him grieved the loss of something he had never had.

Back in their home a moment later, a sob escaped, and then another. George held him, whispering soothing words. When the weight relinquished its hold, Scott felt hallowed out and freer.

George wiped the tears from his cheeks as they held each other. "Feel better?"

Scott considered it for a long moment. "Yes. Yes, I do." He kissed George, tasting his own salty tears. "What do you think Asmodeus meant by 'fate has spoken'?"

George chuckled and glanced down at his belly. "We'll find out in a few months' time."

"What..." Scott glanced down, wide-eyed as his brain caught up. "No... holy crap... how... what... I'm gonna faint."

Scooped off the floor in a move that would never grow old. "Don't worry, I got you."

A baby.

We're having a baby.

A Baby.

Scott's demon laughed his blue ass off. *Thank the demon realm, the demon is finally out of the bag. Or will it be a bear?*

Epilogue

Asmodeus

Asmodeus had enough. The only interesting part of the visit thus far was Scott's arrival with his blissful one, who smelled of something that was unmistakable to Asmodeus.

The bear has been to the forest.

Yes.

He's been in his company… today.

Yes.

I want to see him.

We saw him only last month. The draw—*connection, stop lying to yourself*—was worse than it had ever been. His demon and human side fought continually of late, and it was getting very wearing.

He focused his gaze back on the couple, looking for a distraction. He had never understood how these two ass-holes had created a son like Scott. The demon worked hard, kept his nose clean, and didn't cause Asmodeus any problems, just how he liked it. The problem was the old established demon families; they believed they mattered more than they did. That what happened centuries ago, should continue. Their entitled asses were owed nothing. They had not worked for their position or money, they in-herited it. Their match was that of a pair looking to create a merger between strong bloodlines.

Their strongest bloodline was in the demon who they had shunned for his difference. He would bear them their first grandchild. Asmodeus had felt life growing inside Scott. This pair would be lucky to ever see it. The life was already strong and pure of heart. It would be a force to be reck-oned with once grown. His foresight could see beyond the now, only never when it came to himself. A gift that was also a curse for him.

No matter the searching he had done, the one answer, until Dakata, eluded him. Was a blissful one, the truth? The heart of what troubled him?

Four demons, four had found their blissful ones in a matter of months. Why was this? Was this what had cast him into a purgatory of his own making? A touch?

Centuries ago, he had sought answers to one question. The one that would explain the hold on his soul. For a time, he'd lost all hope of ever escaping his own prison. Yet, here he was, witnessing the truth behind Fate's choices for demons. And why, when most of the time, Asmodeus didn't involve himself in such pettiness as he witnessed here, he would intervene. Just not in the way Randal and Olivia wanted.

The silence left in the wake of Scott, after his declaration and threat, which Asmodeus chose to ignore for now, was deafening.

"Why do you believe Fate is wrong?" he questioned, sounding bored, but it was a façade. He was interested in the answer. The historians had never clarified, satisfactorily, the facts behind a blissful one. Or not in a way that made sense to someone as analytical as Asmodeus. A thinker, he needed to fully grasp the meaning of something before he came to a conclusion.

Randal, not one to read the room, glowered at him, looking down his pointy nose despite the height difference between them. "That creature isn't worthy of our name. Our connections within this realm. Fate should have nothing to do with that. I am part of one of the oldest demon families in the realm, I'll have you know."

"I see," he said flatly. Asmodeus' family was the oldest bloodline in the demon realm he'd discovered in his quest for information.

"Yes. Can't you see that by mixing races in this way, the bloodlines will become weaker?" His expression was haughty as he paced in front of Asmodeus. In his perfect suit, his hair was coiffed so not a strand was out of place. Shoes that shone enough to catch a reflection, he looked nothing like the demon he professed to want to protect, that he never allowed out.

Asmodeus's eyes narrowed in warning. "Yet, here you stand, dressed and acting as your human half."

His demon side had forbidden him to shift into his human form unless...

"What is wrong with that?" he spluttered, while Olivia paled.

"Is it not a double standard, when you stand here before me talking of weakening bloodlines and other hokum, when you act like a petty human who can't get his own way? Did you take the time to get to know George? Find out about his pure bloodline? No. He is classed as one of the highest pedigrees. One who is the only remaining true pureblood bear shifter from a clan that is older than your family line."

"He is of no importance. None."

Asmodeus' lips curled in distaste at the lack of acknowledgment that they had made a mistake. "You have no interest in anything beyond that of your own nose, and that is what is wrong with your argument," he snarled.

Randal coughed violently, his features reddening. "I—"

"Enough." The whiplash of his tone brought stillness from the couple, and rightly so. "Do not bother me again with your petty nonsenses."

He translocated back to his personal chamber, striding over to the stone sitting on a cushion at his bedside. He resisted a heartbeat before he reached to clasp it in his fist. His eyes shut at the familiar feel and warmth against his skin, his pulse accelerated with the knowledge of what he would see when his eyes flickered open. He resisted once more, aware it was futile, as he opened his eyes to look within the visual portable the stone afforded him. His breath caught at the vision before him.

Naked and aroused the man lay with his eyes shut, his hand stroking his cock. The head glistened in the flames of the candles flickering around the bed. A trembly moan came from who Asmodeus couldn't say. His gaze riveted to the hand touching what he wanted. What he denied himself.

Full lips parted, and a whisper followed. "Watch me."

He couldn't stop. Nothing, not even a threat to life could make him turn away as sweat sheened the bronze skin. As the speed of the hand stroking the shaft increased, the eyes opened and met his. The moment, despite the distance, came with an intensity that continued to surprise Asmodeus, as ribbons of cum splattered the fluttering chest.

He could smell the cum, imagine the taste on his tongue. Almost like he'd projected his thought, the man ran a lazy finger through the cum and brought it to his lips to taste. His gaze held Asmodeus captive, as they had the first time he'd seen those eyes in the forest.

His own arousal scented the air, and he moaned in distress, dropping the stone on his bed. His fingers pressed into his eyes as if to banish the image forever burnished in his brain. "When will I find the answer!"

You already have it.

About the Author
Lisa Oliver

Lisa Oliver lives in the wilds of New Zealand, although her beautiful dogs Hades and Zeus are now living somewhere else far more remote than she is. Reports indicate they truly enjoy chasing possums although they still can't catch them. In the meantime, Lisa is living a lot closer to all her adult kids and grandchildren which means she gets a lot more visitors. However, it doesn't look like she's ever going to stop writing - with over a hundred paranormal MM (and MMM) titles to her name so far, she shows no signs of slowing down.

When Lisa is not writing, she is usually reading with a cup of tea always at hand. Her grown children and grandchildren sometimes try and pry her away from the computer and have found that the best way to do it is to promise her chocolate. Lisa will do anything for chocolate… and occasionally crackers. She has also started working out, because of the chocolate and the crackers.

Lisa loves to hear from her readers and other writers (I really do, lol). You can catch up with her on any of the social media links below.

I finally got my Patreon page up and running – you can check that out at

Facebook –

Official Author page –

My new private teaser group -

My MeWe Group -

And Instagram -

My blog -

Twitter – _

Email me directly at yoursintuitively@gmail.com.

Other Books By Lisa Oliver

Please note, I have now marked the books that contain mpreg and MMM for those of you who don't like to read those type of stories, or for those who prefer them Hope that helps ☺

Cloverleah Pack

Book 1 – The Reluctant Wolf – Kane and Shawn

Book 2 – The Runaway Cat – Griff and Diablo

Book 3 – When No Doesn't Cut It – Damien and Scott

Book 3.5 – Never Go Back – Scott and Damien's Trip and a free story about Malacai and Elijah

Book 4 – Calming the Enforcer – Troy and Anton

Book 5 – Getting Close to the Omega – Dean and Matthew

Book 6 – Fae for All – Jax, Aelfric and Fafnir (M/M/M)

Book 7 – Watching Out for Fangs –Josh and Vadim

Book 8 – Tangling with Bears – Tobias, Luke, and Kurt (M/M/M)

Book 9 – Angel in Black Leather – Adair and Vassago

Book 9.5 – Scenes from Cloverleah – four short stories featuring the men we've come to love

Book 10 – On the Brink – Teilo, Raff and Nereus (M/M/M)

Book 11 – Don't Tempt Fate – Marius and Cathair

Book 12 – My Treasure to Keep – Thomas and Ivan

Book 13 – Home is Where the Heart is – Wesley and Castor

The Gods Made Me Do It (Cloverleah spin off series)

Book One - Get Over It – Madison and Sebastian's story

Book Two - You've Got to be Kidding – Poseidon and Claude (mpreg)

Book Three – Don't Fight It – Lasse and Jason

Book Four – Riding the Storm – Thor and Orin (mpreg elements [Jason from previous book gives birth in this one])

Book Five – I Can See You – Artemas and Silvanus (mpreg elements – Thor gives birth in this one)

Book Six – Someone to Hold Me – Hades and Ali (mpreg elements but no birth)

Book Seven – You'll Know in Your Heart – Baby and Owen (mpreg)

Book Eight – Worth It – Zeus and Paulie (mpreg)

Book Nine – When Three Points Collide – Ra, Kirill and Arvyn (M/M/M) (mpreg elements, no birth)

Book Ten – Special Enough – Odin and Evan

Book Eleven – Reconciliation: Seth's Story – Seth and Luka (mpreg is a small part of this story)

Book Twelve – Being Loki - Loki and Anubis

Book Thirteen – Give Me A Reason – Helios and Bruno

Book Fourteen – Fenrir's Fate – Fenrir and Dorian

Book Fifteen – Wanting to Belong – Hephaestus and Landyn

The Necromancer's Smile (This is a trilogy series under the name The Necromancer's Smile where the main couple, Dakar and Sy are the focus of all three books – these cannot be read as standalone).

Book One – Dakar and Sy – The Meeting

Book Two – Dakar and Sy – Family affairs

Book Three – Dakar and Sy – Taking Care of Business

Bound and Bonded Series

Book One – Don't Touch – Levi and Steel

Book Two – Topping the Dom – Pearson and Dante

Book Three – Total Submission – Kyle and Teric

Book Four – Fighting Fangs – Ace and Devin

Book Five – No Mate of Mine – Roger and Cam

Book Six – Undesirable Mate – Phillip and Kellen

Stockton Wolves Series

Book One – Get off My Case – Shane and Dimitri

Book Two – Copping a Lot of Sin – Ben, Sin and Gabriel (M/M/M)

Book Three – Mace's Awakening – Mace and Roan

Book Four – Don't Bite – Trent and Alexi

Book Five – Tell Me the Truth – Captain Reynolds and Nico (mpreg)

Alpha and Omega Series

Book One – The Biker's Omega – Marly and Trent

Book Two – Dance Around the Cop – Zander and Terry

Book Three – Change of Plans - Q and Sully

Book Four – The Artist and His Alpha – Caden and Sean

Book Five – Harder in Heels – Ronan and Asaph

Book Six – A Touch of Spring – Bronson and Harley

Book Seven – If You Can't Stand the Heat – Wyatt and Stone (Previously published in an anthology)

Book Eight – Fagin's Folly – Fagin and Cooper

Book Nine – The Cub and His Alphas – Daniel, Zeke and Ty (MMM)

Book Ten – The One Thing Money Can't Buy – Cari and Quaid

Book Eleven – Precious Perfection – Devyn and Rex

Book Twelve – More Than a Handful - Karl and Tanner

Spin off from The Biker's Omega – BBQ, Bikes, and Bears – Clive and Roy

Balance – Angels and Demons

The Viper's Heart – Raziel and Botis

Passion Punched King – Anael and Zagan

Soul Deep – Uriel and Haures

Found – Raphael and Seir

Demon Masks and Angel Wings – Michael and Orobas

Love Before Time – Lucifer and Gabriel

Arrowtown

A Tiger's Tale – Ra and Seth (mpreg)

Snake Snack – Simon and Darwin (mpreg)

Liam's Lament – Liam Beau and Trent (MMM) (Mpreg)

Doc's Deputy – Deputy Joe and Doc (Mpreg)

Cam's Chance – Cam and Fergus (Mpreg)

Stone Cold Obsidian – Dian and Kee (Mpreg)

Brutus's Surprise – Brutus and Heath

Hal's Silence – Hal and Blade (mpreg although not the main focus of the story)

Ness's Wait – Ness and Cyrus (mpreg)

City Dragons

Dragon's Heat – Dirk and Jon

Dragon's Fire – Samuel and Raoul

Dragon's Tears – Byron and Ivak

The Magic Users of Greenford – a new trilogy.

Book One - Illuminate

Book Two – Eradicate

Book Three – Validate

Words Not Necessary – Rocky and Neo – a spin off short story from this world.

My Arranged Marriage Fantasy Romance Books (not Fated Mates)

The Infidelity Clause – Nikolas and Caspian

Don't Judge A Prince by his Undergarments – Mintyn and Syrius

An Article of Lies – Xavier and Remy

The Pirate's Treasure – Rojan and Petrov

A Marriage of Necessity – Jasper and Avalon

Six Types of Apology – Vincent and Orion

Quirk of Fate

Summons – Edward and Mammon

Reggie's Reasons – Reggie and Dirkin

The Mating of Blind Billy Hipp – Billy and Dathan

Demon Dabbling – Zese and Percy

Quirk of Fates Shorts

Saving Moses – Tucker and Moses

Catching Damont – Damont and Rebel

Not A Typical Meet Cute – Locryn and Zac

Hellhound Collar Series

Collar and Scruff (Prequel) – Raoul and Jason

Better Than Sweets (Book 1) – Java and Cyril

Precious Blue (Book 2) – Beau and Blue (mpreg elements in last chapter.)

Cain's Shadow – Cain and Ollie (mpreg)

Cooking With Magic – Faron and Patrick

Assassin's Alley

Not that Kind of Demon – Python and Cyrus

Sweet Things for a Crocodile – Storm and Pax

Benedict and Bear Trilogy

Benedict and Bear #1 – Benedict and Dixon

Benedict and Bear #2 – What's Done is Done

Tangled Tentacles – in Collaboration with JP Sayle

Book one – Alexi – Alexi and Danik

Book 2 – Victor – Azim and Victor (mpreg)

Book 3 – Todd – Todd, Lucas, and Ki – MMM (mpreg)

Book 4 – Markov – Markov and Cassius

Book 5 – Kelvin – Kelvin and Magnus (mpreg - Markov)

Assassins To Order With JP Sayle

Marvin – Marvin and Ajani

Ben – Ben, Nico, and Teilo (MMM)

The Baby Question – a short story catching up with men from the Tangled Tentacles and Assassin series (MM, MMM and Mpreg)

Duron – Duron and Beaumont

Conrad – Conrad and Kylo (mpreg elements)

Dancing With The Devil – Wyatt and James (mpreg)

Standalone:

I Should've Stayed Home: Irwin's Story – Part of the Nocturne Bay collab series – Irwin and Kolton

The Fall of the Fairy Tale Prince – Charlie and Lex (A spin off from Dancing Around the Cop and Change of Plans in the A&O series)

Stay True to Me – Con and Ven

Rowan and the Wolf – Rowan and Shadow

Bound by Blood – Max and Lyle – (a spin off from Cloverleah Pack #7)

The Power of the Bite – Dax and Zane

One Wrong Step – Robert and Syron

Uncaged – Carlin and Lucas (Shifter's Uprising in conjunction with Thomas Oliver)

Also under the penname Lee Oliver/Lisa Oliver

Northern States Pack Series

Book One – Ranger's End Game – Ranger and Aiden

Book Two – Cam's Promise – Cam and Levi

Book Three – Under Sean's Protection – Sean and Kyle

Book Four – Newton's Law – Newton and Tron

About the Author JP Sayle

Eccentric cake lover who has a passion for words of all kinds. I'm Jayne or JP, I live in the Isle of Man. A tiny place in the Irish sea where all the magic happens. I'm a confessed bookaholic and if I'm not writing I love to snuggle with a book or two…if you catch my drift.

If you're interested in keeping up to date, then I've a few places you can do that, and they're listed below. My website is where you'll find all the different Me's there are, LOL. As I travel this path into the future, I'm going to be writing in different genres so to stop there being any confusion I'll be writing under different pen names.

If you would like to give me any feedback or just have any questions, go ahead and friend me on Facebook, and I would be happy to answer anything. I hope you enjoyed this book and if you would also like to leave a review, then I would love to read your thoughts. Even if you just want to rate it, I'll be grateful

Thank you for being a part of my dream.

Goodreads

Tumblr

Bookbub

Instagram

Facebook

Facebook Author
page

JP Manx Minx's

Other Books by JP Sayle

Standalone

When Fake Changed Everything

Christmas beyond Christmas

The Elves and the Bondage Daddy)

Agrippa My Heart

His Boy to Tease

Headshot

A Brat For Kinkmas

Hanging With Daddy

A Little Christmas Matty Secret

A Little Christmas Terrence

Music & Dreams

A Sucker For Christmas

Sweet Haven

Cruising Right Into Love

A Little Christmas Ollie

Series

Assassins To Order With Lisa Oliver

Marvin – Marvin and Ajani in Audio

Ben – Ben, Teilo & Nico in Audio

Duron – Duron & Beaumont

Conrad – Conrad & Kylo

Dancing With the Devil – Wyatt & James

Tangled Tentacles Series with Lisa Oliver

Alexi #1in audio

Victor #2 in audio

Todd #3 in audio

Markov # 4in audio

Kelvin # 5 in audio

Obsessions Series with Lisa Oliver

Demon's Obsession

Controller's Obsession

Christa's Obsession out Feb 2025

Secretary's Obsession out March 2025

King's Obsession out May 2025

Little Paws Haven Series

Little Treasure he Hides

Little & Lethal

Enforcers Little Warrior coming April 2025

Divergent Omegaverse Series

Alphas Divergent Omega

Taylin's Temptation due Oct 2024

Booker's Bliss due Jan 2025

Spin off Series in the Divergent Omegaverse Darling Ranch

Ranch-Down coming Feb 2025

The Potters Creek Series

A Christmas Wish (book one)

The App Series

The App: Daddy kink (book one)

The App: Littles (book two)

The App: Puppy play (book three)

The Flamingo Bar Series

Always More (book one)

The Little Side of Me (book two)

3 Is the Magic Number (book three)

La Trattoria Di Amore Series

Puzzle Pieces (book one)

Dominated but not Subdued (book two)

Made to Submit

The Playroom Series

Mine, Body and Soul: Part One

Mine, Body and Soul: Part Two

Mine, Body and Soul: Part Three

Ferron's Journey: Damaged Part One (book four)

Ferron's Journey: Hidden Part Two (book five)

Ferron's Journey: Revelation Part Three (book six)

Mine, Body and Soul Trilogy

Ferron's Journey Trilogy

Spinoff Love's Heart Print

Dark River Stone Collective Series

The Light Beneath the Dark (Book One)

When Darkness Turns to Light (Book Two)

Running From Darkness (Book Three)

The Billionaire Playground Series

Property of a Billionaire (Book one)

Reluctant Billionaire (Book two)

Billionaire's Muse (Book three)

Heart Stones Series

.

Blood King

The Manx Cat Guardians Series

Where it all Began: Origins (Book 1)
Seeing Beyond the Scars (Book 2)
Destiny Collides Past and Present (Book 3)
Searching for a Soul to Love (Book 4)
The 12 Disasters of Christmas (Book 5)
Laws of Attraction (Book 6)
The Teacher's Boy (Book 7)
Boxset

Weird & Wacky Shifters

All he wants is a Fingerling

Alphas Fingerling Surprize

A Boy Called Blu

The Rhubarb Effect spin off from Weird & Wacky Shifters

Sticky For You

Rhubarb 2 Go

Ravished By the Rhubarb

Embracing The Stalk

Audio Books

Mine, Body and Soul, Part One: The Playroom Series

Mine, Body and Soul, Part Two: The Playroom Series

Mine, Body and Soul, Part Three: The Playroom Series

Daddy Kink: The App (book one)

Always More: The Flamingo Bar (book one)

When Fake Changed Everything

Ferron's Journey: Damaged Part One

Ferron's Journey: Hidden Part Two

Ferron's Journey: Revelation Part Three

Romance books in a mixed series of M/F and M/M by the Author under a different pen name Jayne Paton

Smith's Corner

Delilah & Dallas (book one)

Layla & Levi (Book two)

Ash & Alora (Book three)

Fox & Faith (book four)

Storm & Stone (book five)

Hunter & Holden (book six)

Crime and Thrillers by the Author under a different pen name J Paton

Headspace

Chozen: Dark MM Crime Drama (Headspace Book 1)

Chozen: Dark MM Crime Drama (Headspace Book 2)